About Fiona Harper

As a child, Fiona Harper was constantly teased for either having her nose in a book, or living in a dream world. Things haven't changed much since then, but at least in writing she's found a use for her runaway imagination. After studying dance at university, Fiona worked as a dancer, teacher and choreographer, before trading in that career for video-editing and production. When she became a mother she cut back on her working hours to spend time with her children, and when her littlest one started pre-school she found a few spare moments to rediscover an old but not forgotten love—writing.

Fiona lives in London, but her other favourite places to be are the Highlands of Scotland, and the Kent countryside on a summer's afternoon. She loves cooking good food and anything cinnamon-flavoured. Of course she still can't keep away from a good book, or a good movie—especially romances—but only if she's stocked up with tissues, because she knows she will need them by the end, be it happy or sad. Her favourite things in the world are her wonderful husband, who has learned to decipher her incoherent ramblings, and her two daughters.

TM

Praise for Fiona Harper

Dancing with Danger

Fiona Harper

First published in Great Britain 2012
by Mills & Boon, an imprint of Harlequin (UK) Limited.
Harlequin (UK) Limited, Eton House, 18-24 Paradise Road,
Richmond, Surrey TW9 1SR

© Fiona Harper 2012

ISBN: 978 0 263 22671 3

Also by Fiona Harper

Swept Off Her Stilettos
Three Weddings and a Baby
Christmas Wishes, Mistletoe Kisses
Blind-Date Baby
Invitation to the Boss's Ball
Housekeeper's Happy-Ever-After
The Bridesmaid's Secret

Did you know these are also available as eBooks?
Visit www.millsandboon.co.uk

To Tammy, a woman of both inner and outer grace,
and an amazing friend. Thank you.

CHAPTER ONE

THE noise of the helicopter's rotor blades made chit-chat impossible. Just as well, really, because Finn had no idea what to say to the tiny woman sitting next to him. Her eyes were wide, her knees clamped together, and her claw-like fingers clutched onto her seat belt as if it were a lifeline.

What on earth had Simon done?

I've found a fabulous replacement for Anya Pirelli, his producer had said. *Just you wait! A real coup!*

Finn knew sales patter when he heard it and after seeing the goods on offer he wasn't sure he was buying. She certainly wouldn't have been his choice for a celebrity guest star.

She was tiny, this woman. A ballet dancer, Simon had said. If they were standing she'd barely reach his shoulders. Nothing like the Amazonian tennis player, with her sporty curves and long blond hair, who was supposed to have been sitting beside him.

No, this woman was so thin she was hardly there. Would probably blow away in a stiff breeze...

Thinking of high winds, he turned to look past the pilot's head through the windshield. The meteorological report had said the storm would hit in the small hours of the morning, but it seemed that the fickle tropical weather had decided to kick up a spectacular welcome for them. A greyish-purple cloud hung on the horizon and the sea below the helicopter was rapidly turning dark and choppy.

The pilot was also frowning and he turned to Finn and shook his head before focusing once again on the darkening sky.

Unfortunately, Finn knew exactly what that meant. He unbuckled his seat belt and reached for his rucksack. Twenty quid said the ballerina baulked at this latest development and he'd be making his way to their temporary desert island home with only Dave the cameraman for company.

Seriously? Had Simon really thought this woman—this girl, almost—was suitable for a gritty survival skills TV programme? He caught Dave's eye. They both looked at the tiny, clenched woman sitting between them, then back at each other. It seemed Finn wasn't the only one who thought Simon's efforts at scraping the bottom of the celebrity barrel for Anya's replacement had been unsuccessful.

The camera operator began to move, too, making sure he had all his equipment with him. A fuller crew would be arriving by much more civilised means later, but for now they only needed Dave, who was used to haring around after Finn and doing daft things. Despite his grumbling to the contrary, Finn was sure Dave secretly loved it.

The tiny ballerina was watching them as if she'd never seen anyone load a rucksack before. She was completely still, and the only parts of her that moved were her eyes, which darted between him and the cameraman.

'What's happening?' she asked. But Finn didn't hear the words; he just saw her mouth move.

He pointed emphatically to the dark clouds hovering over the island getting ever larger on the horizon and yelled at the top of his voice. 'Storm's closing in. We have to move now.'

Her mouth moved again. He was pretty sure she'd just echoed his last word back to him.

'Now,' he said, nodding.

She was lucky. If he'd been on his own he'd have jumped into the water, the helo still moving. But it was too dangerous for a novice. They *would* have to jump, but onto the wetter end of a wide beach. Not quite the luxury of a slow and steady descent on ropes as he'd planned. But there was one thing he could rely on in his life, and on his TV show—hardly anything went to plan. And that was just the way he liked it.

Finn prodded the ballerina's seat belt buckle. She just clutched onto it harder, almost glaring at him.

'Two minutes,' he mouthed, and pointed sharply downward.

None of her features moved, not even her tightly puckered eyebrows, but her expression changed somehow. Something about the eyes—which he noticed were the colour the sea below them would have been if not for the storm. Bright, liquid-blue. The concern in their depths melted into panic.

Now, Finn wasn't an unsympathetic man, but he didn't have time to puppy-walk this girl. The helicopter needed to be well out of range by the time the storm hit. He just didn't have the time to spoon-feed her the confidence she needed. The only course open to him was one of tough love.

'Undo your buckle,' he yelled, miming the action with his fingers. She hesitated, but he couldn't have that. He yelled again, even as compassion tugged at him—told him to ease up. He batted it away, knowing from his days in the army that if he showed any kind of sympathy she might waver. Or freeze. Or panic.

He couldn't have any of those things. The lives of the chopper crew could depend on it.

Fear was still swirling in her eyes, and she didn't tear her gaze from his, but her fingers fumbled with the buckle and eventually it came free.

Good girl.

He shut that thought down before it showed on his face. He'd tell her later, when it was over. He used the same method of walking her through all the steps ready for their insertion as they hurtled towards their destination. He yelled; she obeyed. It was all good.

It seemed like an age before the helicopter was hovering only ten feet above the beach they'd be making their home for the next week. He jumped out of the open-sided helicopter without thinking, letting his knees bend, and rolled before standing up again. A Dave-sized thud beside him told him there was only one passenger left to disembark.

He turned back to the helicopter. She was standing in the doorway, her knuckles whitening on the edges. She didn't look as if she was in a hurry to let go. Too bad.

'Jump!' he yelled, and thrust his arms up and forwards.

Almost instantly he was hit full-force by a flying ballerina. She must have flung herself out the moment he'd spoken, and he'd expected to have to yell at least once more. It took him totally by surprise, causing him to lose his footing, and they both went crashing to the ground. He was only half aware of the blurred shape of the helicopter moving away and the roar of its blades quietening.

He lay there, breathing hard. Damp sand cooling his back and a shaking ballerina warming his front.

'S-sorry,' she stammered. She didn't move, though. Must be too shocked. Or mortified.

She needn't have worried. Finn liked surprises. They produced a delicious little cocktail of adrenalin and endorphins that he'd decided he rather liked. Even when surprises came in the shape of flying ballerinas. He suddenly saw the funny side, and chuckled deep down in his torso.

'What did you say your name was?' he asked the unblinking pair of azure eyes just centimetres from his own.

'Alle—' she croaked out. And then she tried again. 'Allegra.'

Finn grinned at her.

'Well, Allie—Allegra—whoever you are…' He lifted her

off him with surprising ease and dumped her on the sand beside him. He really *would* have to anchor her to a tree if the wind picked up, wouldn't he? Then he jumped to his feet and offered her his hand, grinning even wider. The sky was steel-grey and from the taste of the wind now whipping her long dark ponytail into her face he knew torrential rain was only minutes away.

'Welcome to paradise,' he said.

CHAPTER TWO

Forty-eight hours earlier

ALLEGRA stood rigid in the wings as the corps de ballets rushed past her and onto the stage of the Royal Opera House. *Breathe,* she reminded herself. *Relax. You've done these steps a thousand times in rehearsal. Your body knows what to do. Trust it.*

Too late for more rehearsal now. She'd be on stage in a matter of minutes.

Even so, she couldn't stop herself marking the opening sequence on the spot, her arms and legs carving tiny, precise arcs in the air as they mirrored the full-blown sequence of turns and jumps in her head.

Frustrated, she stopped herself mid-movement, pulled her cardigan off and dumped it somewhere she'd be able to find it later before resuming her position in the wings. As she listened to the orchestra and watched the corps de ballet set the scene, she arched one foot then the other, pressing her shoes into the floor until there was a tight but pleasing stretch in her instep.

Pretend it's just the dress rehearsal. Just another run-though.

She tried very hard to do just that but the adrenalin skipping through her system called her a liar.

Not just a rehearsal, but opening night.

No familiar role, either. Neither for dancers nor audience.

This was a brand new role created just for her. Created to prove the child prodigy, the 'baby ballerina' hadn't lost her sparkle after seven long years in the profession. This new ballet, *The Little Mermaid*, was supposed to silence the critics who'd been prophesying for years now that Allegra Martin would burn brightly and then, just as quickly, burn out.

They'd been saying that since she'd turned twenty and now—three years past that sell-by date—she was sensing the creeping inevitability of that prediction every time she put on her pointe shoes. She almost dreaded sliding her feet into them these days.

Not tonight. It couldn't be tonight. Her father would be devastated.

To distract herself from these unwanted thoughts, she checked her costume. No stiff tutu for this role. Her dress was soft and flowing, ending just below her knees. Layers of chiffon in deep blue, aquamarine and turquoise. And her dark hair, instead of being pulled into its habitual bun, was loose and flowing round her shoulders; only two small sections at the front were caught back to keep it off her face. She resisted the urge to fiddle with the grips, knowing it would probably only make things worse.

The orchestra began a new section of music. It wasn't long now. She should try and focus, slow her butterfly-wing breaths and let her ribs swell with oxygen. She closed her eyes and concentrated on pulling the air in and releasing it slowly.

Behind her eyelids an image gatecrashed her efforts at calm and inner poise. A pair of dark masculine eyes that crinkled at the corners as an unseen mouth pulled them into a smile. She snapped her own eyes open.

Where had that come from?

Now her heart was beating double speed. Damn. She

needed to get her thoughts under control. Less than a minute and she'd be making her entrance. She shook her head and blew out some air.

And then it happened again. With her eyes open.

But this time she saw the smile beneath the eyes. Warm and bright and just a little bit cheeky.

It must be the stress.

Weeks of preparing for this moment had finally got to her. She'd heard other dancers mention the strange random thoughts that plagued them before a performance, but it had never happened to her before. No sudden musings on what she was going to have for dinner that evening or whether she'd remembered to charge her mobile phone.

But why was she thinking of *him?*

A man she didn't even know.

What was he doing here, invading her thoughts at such a crucial moment? It was most unsettling. The last thing she needed right now. And she really meant *right now.* The violins had just picked up the melody that signalled her entrance.

Thankfully, her body had been rehearsed so hard the steps were almost a reflex and it sprang to life and ran onto the stage, dragging her disjointed head with it. There was a moment of hush, a pause in the music, and she sensed every person in the audience had simultaneously and unconsciously held their breath.

They were watching her. Waiting for her.

It was her job to dazzle and amaze, to transport them to another world. And, just as she lifted her arm in a port de bras that swept over her head, preparing her for a series of long and lilting steps across the diagonal of the stage, she wished that were possible. She wished that she *could* escape into another world. And maybe stay there. Somewhere new, somewhere exciting, where no one expected anything of her and she had no possibility of failing to make the grade.

But tonight, while she made the audience believe she was

the Little Mermaid, while they saw her float and turn and defy gravity, she would know the truth. She would feel the impact of every jump in her whole skeleton. She would hear the knocking of her pointe shoes on the stage even if the orchestra drowned out the noise for the audience. She would feel her toes rub and blister inside their unforgiving, solid shoes.

No, she knew the reality of ballet. It might look effortless from the outside, but from the inside it was hard and demanding. It was beautiful, but it wasn't pretty or nice. A fierce kind of beauty that asked for your very soul in return for greatness, and then devoured it without compunction.

She had chosen this path and there was no escape. There *was* no other world. It was all an illusion.

But she would fool them all. She would dance like a girl who was full of sadness, trapped in a state of endless longing, wishing for a reality that could never be hers. And she would dance it well. She wouldn't even be acting, because it was the truth. Her truth.

No escape. No matter how much you wanted it.

Truth like the pain of a thousand knives.

'It was marvellous, darling. Absolutely stunning.'

Allegra air-kissed the woman whose name she couldn't remember and smiled back. 'Thank you. But, really, the credit has to go to Damien, for giving me such wonderful choreography to work with.'

Bad form for a principal dancer to hog all the credit. She was merely the vessel for someone else's genius, after all. The blank canvas for someone else to paint their vision on.

'Nonsense,' the woman said, waving her glass of champagne and spilling a drop on the arm of one of the other guests. Neither one noticed. But Allegra saw it all. She saw every last detail of the after-show party in crisp, exquisite, painful detail.

She saw the Victorian steel and glass arches of the tall hall that had once been part of Covent Garden's famous flower market, the white vertical struts and pillars so straight, so uniform that it felt they were penning her in. She saw the herds of people milling, champagne classes pinched between their fingers, half of them trying to gawp at her while not getting caught. Most of all she saw the tempting patches of midnight-blue beyond the glass and white-painted iron-work of the roof.

If colours could talk, she mused, blue would be an invitation.

Come to me…

She wrenched her eyes off the night sky with difficulty and focused them back where they were supposed to be. 'Excuse me,' she said, bestowing the woman with a gracious smile. 'I see my father over there…'

The woman glanced over her shoulder to where her father was half-hidden by the ostentatious champagne bar filling the middle of the room and then smiled widely back at Allegra. 'Of course, of course. Such a talented conductor and a wonderful man… And it must be fantastic to know that your father is close by on an opening night. What a marvellous sense of support he must give you.'

Allegra wanted to say, *No, actually, it isn't.* She wanted to say that sometimes, having a parent so invested in one's life was anything *but* comforting. She wanted to shock the woman by telling her how many times she'd wished her father was a builder or a schoolteacher. Anything but a conductor. Or how much she wished he'd sit in the back of the stalls occasionally, as the other parents did, rather than standing only a few feet beyond the footlights. Maybe then she wouldn't feel weighed down by his gaze, weighed down by all the hopes and expectations of not just a parent but also her manager and her mentor.

She didn't say anything, of course, but smiled softly in

what the woman probably took for gracious agreement, then used the excuse of her fabulous father to make her departure.

Of course, the press loved the father-daughter angle—devastated widower conducts as ballerina daughter tops the bill, just as he'd done for her tragic mother when she'd been alive. They ate it up.

In her darker moments she silently accused him of loving it, too, of wanting double the glory. Double the adoration. But it wasn't that, really. He just wanted things to be the way they'd been before, wanted to claw back time and resurrect the dead. Impossible, of course, so he'd had to settle for second best. Even so, Allegra hadn't failed to see how he'd come back to life when she'd grown old enough to fill her mother's shoes, dance her mother's old roles.

But not tonight. This one was all hers. No comparisons could be made. She would stand or fall in her own right when the reviews came out in the morning.

She supposed that since she'd used her father as an excuse she'd better go and say hello, so she forged through the crowd, ignoring the people who tried to catch her eye. And there were plenty. She was the star of the show. It was *her* evening, after all.

But she didn't want to talk to them. Not the ones she knew in the company who either envied or idolised her, nor the ones she didn't know, who saw her as some strange creature imbued with magical powers. Gifted—or should that be cursed?—with a talent they daren't even dream of having. They looked at her as if she was somehow different from them. As if she were an alien from outer space. Something to be studied and discussed and dissected. But not human. Never human.

What she wouldn't give for one person on this planet to see past the tutus and the pointe shoes.

More than once she had to change direction when a gap between bodies closed up. Eventually, she just stood still and waited. Chasing the holes in the crowd was impossible; she would wait for the tide of bodies to shift once again and let the gaps come to her. Her stillness, however, was just another way to mark herself out from the other guests.

All around her people were celebrating. It had taken an army of people months to prepare for this night, and now they'd pulled it off their relief and joy was spilling out of them in smiles and laughter and excited conversation.

But Allegra felt nothing.

No joy. No bubbling. Nothing inside desperate to spill out of her.

Except, maybe, a desire to scream.

It was funny, really. For a few years now she'd wondered what would happen if one day she did exactly that. What would they all do if the habitually reserved Allegra Martin planted her feet in the centre of the room and split the hub-bub with a scream that had forced its way up from the depths of her soul?

The look on their faces would be priceless.

She treasured this little fantasy, because it had got her through more stuffy cocktail parties, lunches and benefits than she cared to count. Only it didn't seem quite as funny any more, because tonight she felt like making the fantasy a reality. She really felt like doing it for real. In fact, the urge was quickly becoming irresistible, and that was scaring her.

She had to start moving again, keep walking at all costs, even if she ended up momentarily heading away from her father, because she feared that if she paused, that if her two feet stayed grounded for long enough, she might just do it.

Despite her meandering progress across the Floral Hall, she had almost reached her father now. He hadn't noticed her silent zig-zagging approach, however, because he was deep in conversation with the Artistic Director. She heard her name mentioned briefly above the din of the party. Neither man looked happy.

Had she done badly tonight? Had she let them all down? The thought made the panic racing inside her torso double its speed. And that internal momentum had a strange effect: just as she was on the verge of stepping into the circle of their conversation, a gap opened up to her right and, instead of ploughing forward and greeting her father, she took it.

Bizarrely, she found that once she'd started going in that direction she couldn't stop. Not until she'd left the crush of the party far behind, not until she'd run down the minimalist wooden staircase at full pelt, leaving her warm champagne glass on the flat banister at the top, not until she was standing in the foyer. She rushed past the cloakrooms to the large revolving door and moments later she was amidst the pillars and cobbles of Covent Garden, the cold night air soothing her lungs.

But she didn't run any further; she stood there, blinking.

What was she doing?

She couldn't leave yet. She couldn't escape.

Her father would be waiting for her. There were senior staff and investors and a minor Royal waiting to greet her.

No, her body said. *Enough.* And she was inclined to agree with it.

Now that the adrenalin high from the performance had evaporated, she ached all over. She'd been up since six, had done class this morning and then had spent most of the afternoon making last-minute changes to a pas de deux with her partner, Stephen, that the choreographer had insisted were essential. And the performance that had seemed so light and ethereal on the outside had been gruelling beyond belief.

She stood still for a few seconds, closed her eyes. *Trap the breath then let it out slowly...smoothly.*

Unfortunately, a sense of duty was hardwired into a dancer's psyche.

When she had finished pushing the carbon dioxide out through her clenched teeth she opened her lids again.

And then the ballerina turned, with all the grace expected of her, and let the revolving door coax her back inside, let its momentum almost propel her back up the stairs and into the crowded bar. Her glass, full of warm and flat champagne, was waiting for her on the banister and she retrieved it before pulling herself up tall and losing herself in the tangle of bodies.

Allegra cranked open an eyelid and focused half-heartedly on the digital clock by her bedside. Definitely way too late still to be awake. Or should that be way too early to get up?

Ugh. Who cared?

She always got this way after an opening night—too tired, too excited, too aware of the reviews only hours away now in the morning editions.

Knowing she'd only get even more grumpy if she lay there in the dark chasing sleep, she fumbled on the bedside cabinet for the TV remote and then pointed it into the darkness. A bluish light flooded the room. She squinted and drummed repeatedly on the volume button, hushing the garish advert for oven cleaner. She didn't want to wake her father.

She changed the channel a dozen times. And then a dozen times more.

There really was nothing on at this time in the morning, was there? Unless you counted infomercials, 'channel off-air' graphics and lengthy documentaries about long-forgotten prog rock bands. She carried on changing channels until she lost count, and she was just about to give up and turn the TV set off when the image replacing the previous one caused her thumb to freeze above the button.

A pair of crinkling brown masculine eyes. And a killer smile to match.

She held her breath. Then she looked towards her bedroom door and quickly back again to the television. Without tearing her eyes from the screen, she pressed down hard on the volume button until the noise from the set was only just audible, turning the subtitles onto compensate. And then, finally, she let out the air she'd been holding captive in her mouth.

Finn McLeod. My, he was gorgeous!

All rugged male energy, with a glint of adventure in his eyes.

His dark hair, that never seemed to sit quite right, flopped over one side of his forehead and a smile stretched his stubble-studded jaw. She'd had no idea they were showing late-night reruns of *Fearless Finn*. Just as well, really, because if she'd known she could have watched him jumping into rapids and hanging off mountains by his fingertips all night long, she might have done just that. Unfortunately, a sleep-deprived ballerina at the Royal Opera House would not have gone down well.

Sometimes, she thought, as she tugged an extra pillow from beside her and stuffed it behind her shoulders, she felt so old. That wasn't right at twenty-three, was it? But she felt as if she'd been riding the same unrelenting merry-go-round of classes, rehearsals and performances for so long that her life had sped up, and she'd aged faster than she should have done. It was hardly surprising that, deep down, she longed for something fresh, something new.

Her gaze returned to the screen, where Finn McLeod, in his gorgeous, rolling Scottish accent, was explaining how to find food if one was unlucky enough to be stranded in the mountains.

She smiled. Really grinned. See? She'd never realised there were tiny little seeds inside pine cones that could be prised out and eaten.

Or had she?

She supposed she had. She had pine nuts on her pasta all the time. It was just that she'd never connected the tree on the mountainside with the tiny packet on the supermarket shelf, never thought about what bit of the tree the nut came from or how it could be harvested.

And that was why she loved watching *Fearless Finn*. It

reminded her she was *young,* that there was so much of the world she had yet to see, so much to learn about life. The feeling would well up inside her until she wished she could literally climb inside the flickering rectangle on the wall and run down that hillside with him, or taste that pine nut fresh from the cone for herself.

Finn turned to the camera and grinned, getting right up close to the lens, before flinging himself off a rocky river-bank and into the fast-flowing water.

Okay, maybe education about the planet wasn't the *only* reason she watched this show. But he was so…so…

She didn't really know what he was, or exactly how he made her feel, only that she felt alive watching him, that she believed she could sprout wings and fly away when he was on the screen.

Another symptom of the narrow, ultra-focused life one had to live if one was going to get to the top in her profession. Ballet had to be *everything.* So, just as she felt she didn't know much about the big wide world beyond the ballet studio, she didn't really have a lot of experience with men, either.

But seeing that six foot hunk of testosterone and adven-ture, with his unruly dark hair and even unrulier dark eyes, made her want to learn a little more about *both.*

She blushed hard and bit her lip. It seemed her first teen-age crush had finally arrived after a rather lengthy, ballet-related delay.

Well, so what? Everyone had their guilty pleasures, didn't they? Finn McLeod was hers. And until the milk floats began to moan through Notting Hill, outside her father's tall white house, she was going to forget all about ballet and mermaids and morning editions, and lose herself in a pair of captivat-ing brown eyes.

Watching dawn break from the top of a glacier was *definitely* the way Finn McLeod liked to start his day. The horizon had been the clearest, purest cobalt but now as the sun pushed upward it slowly turned an icy, pale blue.

'Wow,' the A-list Hollywood actor who stood beside him said.

Wow, indeed.

'This is, like, perfect,' the guy said, nodding gently.

'Yup,' said Finn. It didn't get much better than this.

He and Tobias Thornton, action movie god, stood there, silent, staring at the awesome display Creation was putting on for them, better than any celluloid car chase or exploding building.

Finn glanced across at the backpacks that were sitting a few feet away on the ice. 'The helicopter will be here shortly,' he said, his gaze drawn inevitably back towards the sunrise. It was swiftly blocked out by six and a half feet of movie star. Finn discovered that was because Toby was intent on crushing the life out of him in a bear hug. Not part of the plan, really, since they'd spent the better part of a week trying to *survive* this frozen wasteland.

'Thanks, man,' Toby said, thumping Finn on the back.

'No problem,' Finn replied, wheezing slightly.

The actor released him and stood back. 'This has been life-changing, Finn. I mean it.' He turned to face the sunrise once again, but carried on talking. 'I feel as if I've stripped away all the garbage from my life and discovered who I really am.'

Finn just nodded. That was what spending a significant chunk of time in the wilderness would do for a man. It was why he loved it here. Or any place a man-made structure, or a power line, or even a mobile phone signal were many, many miles away. It made him feel alive. *Connected* to something indefinable, something bigger than himself.

'I'm never going to be the same, man...'

Finn frowned. Of course, normally he travelled to places like this on his own. He'd planned to enjoy the silence. Not much chance of that now, as his actor friend continued to gush.

But this was what the TV company had wanted. Having a tag-along celebrity for the fifth series of the show hadn't been his idea; he'd been quite happy with the previous format, where he'd spend a week in various remote locations showing the audience not only how to fend for themselves in that environment, but giving them a taste of a rarely seen gem of a place.

But that hadn't been enough for the TV execs. He was too competent, apparently. He grunted out loud at that thought. What rubbish. Being competent at this stuff was why he'd got the job in the first place. Unfortunately, the suits thought the viewing public had got that message now, and were going to get bored with more of the same, so they'd come up with a plan to saddle him with a novice so he could pass on his expertise. And, of course, people loved watching celebs thrown out of their glitzy worlds and into the deep end. What could go wrong? the TV company had said.

Finn sighed. He supposed it hadn't been that awful. The guy standing beside him had been okay company, and it had been fun to watch him build his confidence over the last week. Whether the experience would produce a lasting change in the well-known bad boy and womaniser was another matter altogether.

'So who's your next victim?' the actor said, turning to him.

Finn smiled to himself. 'Anya Pirelli.'

The actor let out a low whistle. 'The tennis player?'

Finn nodded.

Toby slapped him on the back. 'Lucky dog.'

'Just don't tell my fiancée,' he said, grinning.

'You have a fiancée?' Toby pulled a face. 'Too bad, man.'

'Oh, I don't think I'm doing too badly—she's Natalie Cross.'

'The chick who does the nature documentaries?'

Finn nodded, and Toby whistled again. 'Definitely not doing too badly, mate!' and then he frowned. 'But spending a week stranded with Anya Pirelli... She's not the jealous type, is she, your fiancée?'

Finn laughed and shook his head. He'd been joking. Neither of them were jealous types. That was what made them the perfect match. They both liked their freedom and, even though they were committed to each other, they both understood how destructive the urge to pin someone down and keep them for yourself could be.

'When's the wedding?' Toby asked, and Finn stopped smiling.

He shrugged. 'When we get around to it.' They'd been engaged for two years, which seemed a long time to some people, but he and Nat travelled so much for their jobs theirs was almost a long-distance relationship. They'd find a date they could both manage eventually. Just the knowledge they'd agreed to do it some time in the future was enough for now.

'No... Nat will be fine about it,' Finn added.

Toby's eyes glittered wickedly. 'Still, you'll be stuck alone with Anya in the jungle somewhere or up a mountain. Who's to tell?'

Finn gestured over his shoulder to the camera operator who was standing a little way down the slope. 'Who d'you think?'

Toby slapped himself on the forehead. 'I've got so used to them being there, I kind of forgot we weren't on our own.'

Finn shrugged. It was easy enough to do. Sometimes he threw himself headlong into risky situations while filming, completely forgetting he wasn't on his own and that a camera, a producer and possibly a safety expert were trailing along behind him.

He took a few paces away from Toby, tried to create a little bubble of space and silence where he could let all this grandeur and beauty seep into him so it could mingle with all the other memories and experiences he collected on his travels. However, as mind-blowing as each location was, he always felt there was room for more, that a little piece of him ached for the ultimate destination, the ultimate adventure. That was what kept him moving, kept him searching.

There was a glint of silver off to the right in the sky, and Finn lifted his hand to shield his eyes further.

Yep. That was the chopper.

Time for the next adventure. And he couldn't wait.

CHAPTER THREE

A NEAT stack of newspapers sat on the kitchen table in the basement kitchen. Other than the sound of her own breathing, Allegra could hear nothing. She tore her eyes from the stack and looked at her father.

'Shall I read them to you?' he asked.

Allegra shook her head and returned her gaze to the tower of newsprint in front of her. Instead of taking the top one off the pile, she picked one from the middle and eased it from its place. The critic who wrote for that paper was always the hardest to read. Not because he was vicious. He was blunt, yes, but never vicious. It was much, much worse than that.

By some magical power, this man always managed to hone in on those elements of the performance that Allegra fretted about herself and then shone a big, nasty spotlight on them. However, if she could read this review and get it out of the way, the rest would be a piece of cake. At least, that was what she was telling herself.

She pushed the pile of papers to the far edge of the table to give herself space to unfold the broadsheet and carefully turned pages, smoothing each one flat, until she reached the arts section.

There, filling almost half the page, was a grainy black and white photo of her and Stephen in the last act. Stephen, as always, looked like one of those sculpted marble statues, all perfect musculature and good bone structure, as he supported her in an arabesque.

She felt a little of the panic drumming beneath her ribs drain away. She didn't look too bad herself. And the line of that back leg was perfect, even though she'd only hit that position for a split second before moving through it to the next step. Surely, a picture like that had to be a good omen?

She glanced down at the text beneath the picture and phrases swam in front of her eyes.

'Astounding.'

'Technically brilliant.'

'Allegra Martin didn't miss a step...'

She released the breath she'd been holding out through her lips and let it curve them into a slight smile. She risked a look at her father, but he was wading through another of the papers. The cup of chamomile tea he'd made her was now almost cold. She reached for it and took a sip, then grimaced.

Now her initial shakiness had subsided she went back to the beginning of the article and read it in whole sentences, taking it in slowly, weighing every word instead of fracturing it into phrases that had a tendency to jump out at her.

It all sounded good but as she switched from the bottom of the second column to the top of the third she started to feel chilly again. By the time she'd read a couple more paragraphs she knew why.

'I've always been a huge Allegra Martin fan...' the man had written.

The ballerina in question raised an eyebrow. Really? If that was the case, she'd hate to be on his bad side!

'...but while her performance as the Little Mermaid was technically flawless, I still don't think she has lived up to her early promise.'

Allegra's stomach bottomed out and a faint taste of chamomile tea clung to her teeth, making her feel queasy. She read on.

'Miss Martin seems to have lost the engaging sense of wonder and joy she had as a young dancer and, while I appreciate her virtuosity, I don't feel she captured either the exquisite joy of first love nor the torture of unfulfilled longing that a truly great rendition of this part would require.'

She wanted to stop, but she couldn't. It was like driving a speeding car when the brakes had failed. Her brain was frantically pressing on the pedal, but her eyes kept reading.

And it only got worse:

'In Hans Christian Andersen's original story, the Little Mermaid was a creature not blessed with a soul, and I'm afraid, with Allegra Martin in the title role, this was all too obvious.'

Allegra didn't move. Nothing would work. Not her mouth, not her legs, not her arms.

Soulless? He'd called her *soulless?*

She pushed her chair away from the table and stood up, met her father's eyes.

He didn't say anything. Very unusual for her father. He always had something to say about her performances, some aspect she could improve for next time. Also, no matter how hard on her he was in private, when the reviews came in he normally got very defensive, would argue why the writer was wrong.

The chill in her stomach dropped a few degrees.

There was nothing to argue about, nothing to refute. She could see it now—the glimmer of disappointment in his eyes.

'You think it's true, don't you?' she asked, her voice almost a whisper. Even at that volume, it managed to wobble slightly.

He closed and opened his eyes slowly. 'I don't know what's been wrong with you the last year or so, Allegra. You're just not as focused as you used to be. Your work is suffering.'

She looked at him with pleading eyes. Yes, her father was

hard on her, had always pushed her, but he was supposed to be her protector, her champion! Why was he saying this? Why couldn't he dismiss the opinion of one 'know-it-all hack', as he liked to call them?

That was when she saw something else in his eyes, clouding out the original emotion, making it darker and harder. He wasn't just disappointed with her; he was angry.

'You can't waste your gift like this. You've got to stop throwing it all away.'

There was a sharp stinging at the back of Allegra's eyes. He wasn't talking about losing the role of principal dancer—although that might be a possibility if her current artistic drought didn't end—he was talking about the big picture, the vision he'd had for her ever since he'd put her name down for an audition for the Royal Ballet School, aged ten.

He wasn't talking about jobs and salaries and reviews. He was talking about living up to her mother's legacy, of carrying on where Maria Martin had left off on the road to becoming one of the greatest British ballet dancers in history.

He was saying she just wasn't good enough. Might never be.

Allegra rose to her feet, looked at the paper still open on the table and then back at her father.

'I want to see you bringing that same energy and commitment you used to have back to every class, every rehearsal, every performance,' he said. 'You owe it to yourself.'

You owe it to *her*. That was what he really meant, wasn't it?

Didn't he think she would if she could? I'm trying, she wanted to scream at him, but nothing's working because I feel *dead* inside! I'm not her. I haven't got her talent. I'm not sure I've even got my own any more! Or that I want it if I do have it.

The words didn't even get close to being on the tip of her tongue; they swirled around her head instead, making her eyes blur and her throat swell. She licked her dry lips and forced something out.

'I've got class at ten-thirty,' she said. And then, without looking at her father again, she turned and headed up the stairs that led from their basement kitchen, pulled her coat from the hook near the door and walked with silent steps into the chilly morning air.

People were everywhere. Finn stood still and took a few moments to adjust. After a week in the frozen wilderness, where the only noise was the wind curling round rocks or the crunch of snow beneath his boots, a busy provincial airport terminal was an assault on the senses.

Not that he minded.

This was just a different kind of adventure, a different kind of wilderness. One that Finn considered far more dangerous, even with its thick sheen of civilisation.

And, while he hadn't minded Toby's company, he'd been secretly relieved when the man had been whisked away in a limo as soon as their helicopter had hit the tarmac. Now he was alone again. No need to use his vocal cords unless he really wanted to. No need to take anyone else's needs into account. He could move at his own speed and choose his own route.

He ignored the moving walkway, clogged with bored-looking tourists with suitcases, hitched his rucksack higher on his back and set off down the near-empty carpeted area beside it, his strides long and his smile wide.

A buzzing in one of the side pockets of his cargo trousers tickled his legs. At first it made him jump, but then he realised what it was and bent to fish his mobile phone out of a slim pocket low down on his right thigh.

'Hello?'

'Great! Finn, I'm so glad your mobile's finally on again. It's all gone pear-shaped since I last talked to you...'

Finn gave a lopsided smile and began walking again as he waited for his producer to finish his mini-rant. Simon always got like this after a shoot. Finn knew he just had to let Simon vent until he'd either run out of steam or run out of breath—whichever came first.

When the sentences weren't hurtling past at a hundred miles an hour and blurring into each other, Finn firmly squeezed a question of his own in. 'So...what's *really* up, Si?'

There was a slight pause at the other end, as if the other man's unending monologue had suddenly encountered an unexpected hazard and had taken a split second to work out how to flow around it.

'Slight snag, as they say...'

'What sort of snag? We're supposed to be off to Panama tomorrow. Can't it wait until we get back?'

'Ah...'

Okay. Now he'd managed to dry Simon up completely. This was news Finn probably didn't want to hear.

'It's Panama we've got a problem with.'

Finn stopped walking altogether. 'Oh?'

'Anya Pirelli has injured her knee in a training session. Her coach says it's going to be months before she'll be ready to tackle a desert island.'

That wasn't a problem, it was an unexpected blessing! Finn started striding again.

'How awful,' he said, feeling genuinely sorry for Anya, but he couldn't help thinking there was a silver lining.

'Don't worry, though,' Simon added quickly. 'I'm working on a couple of possible replacements as we speak.'

Now, that was what Finn had been afraid of.

'There's no need, Si. We can go back to the old format. Me on my own.'

Simon's silence was heavy enough to slow Finn's pace yet again.

'No can do, I'm afraid, Finn. The TV company have seen the rushes for the first new-format episode. They loved the Formula One star in the swamp. Said it did just what they'd been hoping it would. They're adamant you need a celebrity sidekick.'

'But—'

'I agree with them, Finn. It makes you seem more human. Less of an indestructible force of nature yourself, someone the ordinary guy in the street can relate to.'

Finn had reached the end of the wide hallway now and he had to dodge people stepping off the end of the moving walkway as the space narrowed and funnelled them towards the gates.

'Okay, okay,' he finally said. 'Let me know who you've got lined up when you've got something firm.'

He said his goodbyes and hung up. He was just about to shove his phone back into his khaki pocket and button the flap shut when he realised there was someone else he probably ought to call before he couldn't use it again.

He punched a speed-dial button and waited. He got Nat's voicemail. That was the problem with having a woman in his life who was as free-spirited as he was. He left a brief message, then checked his account for messages, too.

First in the queue was one from Nat.

'Hi, Finn,' her message said, sounding a little tense. 'Look, the South Pacific shoot has been moved forward and I've got to fly out this evening.'

Finn frowned. He hadn't seen her for four weeks, and he'd been hoping to catch up with her this evening. Oh, well. It couldn't be helped.

'Anyway,' Nat continued, 'your itinerary says you're connecting through Schiphol, and so am I. I could get there early and we could meet up.'

Oh. Okay. That would be good.

Finn nodded to himself and waited to see if there was

anything else. The pause was so long he'd started to pull the phone away from his ear when she spoke again.

'Finn, I—' Another pause, shorter this time. 'We really need to talk, that's all. Call me.'

And that was that. Finn tucked the phone back into his thigh pocket and shrugged.

Gate Ten loomed close and he moved swiftly and silently through the forest of people until he was standing near the desk by the doors.

The thought of leaving one point on the planet only to arrive somewhere different a few hours later always got Finn excited. And the sense of anticipation did a good job of stifling any niggling questions trying to take root in his brain. Like whether he should have been a little more heartbroken about not speaking to Nat in person. Or that perhaps he should wonder why she'd slipped from his consciousness as quickly and as completely as the phone bumping against his leg in its khaki pocket.

After class that day Allegra returned home. No one had said anything, but she'd known they'd all read every word of that review. It had been there in the surreptitious glances when they'd thought she wasn't looking. It had been there in the barely contained smirks behind her back. She hadn't even acknowledged the few sympathetic looks that some of the girls had tried to send her. Those had been the worst.

She'd been so much younger than everyone else when she'd joined the company, still a child almost. If the age difference hadn't driven a wedge between her and her contemporaries, her meteoric rise through the ranks in the following couple of years certainly had. Now she had colleagues and dancing partners, but she didn't really have any friends.

All she had was her father.

That was why she headed straight to his study after she'd let herself in. Even though they hadn't argued, there'd been such a horrible atmosphere between them. She'd apologise. She'd make it right again. She'd swallow the rising tide of suffocation and live with it a little longer. Because she understood he didn't mean it really. And he did *try.*

She pushed open the heavy wooden door and looked around. The room was empty. At least, she thought it was. She stepped inside to get a better look.

'Daddy?'

Where was he? She wandered round to the other side of the large cherrywood desk with the green leather top, trailing her fingers along the edge as she did so. One of these days her father would have to give in and learn to use a computer, but for now he was steadfastly holding out. There was no scribbled note, no scrap of paper to hint at where he'd gone or when he might be back. She sighed.

Oh, well. She'd just have to find him later. She had a rehearsal in an hour and it had been tight fitting in a trip back home as it was.

She had reached the other side of the desk again when the phone rang. By the time she reached the door the answerphone kicked in and a male voice filled the empty room.

'Hi. This is Simon Tatler again. I was wondering if you'd had a chance to think over the offer for Miss Martin to appear on *Fearless Finn.* As you know, the schedule is pretty tight, so could you possibly get back to me today?'

He added his number and email address and rang off.

Allegra stood, half in, half out of her father's study with her mouth open.

An invitation to appear on *Fearless Finn!* A warm feeling surged up from her toes and burst up through her, leaving a smile on her lips. She'd get to meet him? Actually stand face to face with him? Her heart began to pound at the thought.

And then her excitement began to evaporate. This Simon had phoned before? Why was this the first she'd heard of it?

Her father found her moments later in the doorway, frowning. She jumped when he lightly touched her on the shoulder.

'Are you okay, Allegra?'

On autopilot, Allegra nodded, but then she realised what
she was doing. She turned to face him.

'What was that message about? The one about *Fearless
Finn?*'

Her father looked puzzled. 'Who?'

'The TV show...'

He blinked and shook his head faintly. 'Nothing, really.
They were looking for a celebrity guest. I tried to tell the man
you couldn't do it, but he insisted I think about it.'

'*You* think about it?'

Her father nodded. 'Yes.'

Allegra's eyebrows pinched together. 'Don't you mean, he
suggested *I* think about it?'

He shrugged and walked past her into the study. 'It hardly
warrants an argument over semantics, Allegra. You simply can't do it. They wanted you to fly out to some god-
forsaken place tomorrow and stay there for seven nights. I
don't know what the man was thinking even approaching
us about it—'

'And you didn't think to tell me about this?'

Her father smiled at her. That same soft smile he'd given
her when she'd been a little girl and had tried to use a complicated word and had got it wrong.

'I didn't see the need.' He walked round to the other side
of the desk and rifled through some papers, effectively dis-
missing her. 'As I said, it was impossible.'

'I know it's impossible!' She paused and cleared her
throat, got control of herself. 'But that's not the point,' she
said evenly. 'It's *my* career. It was my decision. You should
at least have mentioned it to me.'

Her father looked up, a wad of papers clutched in his hand, looking perplexed.

He just didn't get it, did he? It didn't matter what she said, or what she did; he would never get it.

To him, she was just another thing to be conducted. He waved his baton and she jumped. He waved it again and she stayed silent. And she'd let him. All these years she'd let him, because she'd seen what he'd become after his wife had died, how he'd almost given up on everything. And she'd seen his renaissance when she'd started to excel at her mother's art. How could she snatch that back from him and still live with herself?

She continued to stare at her father, who had paused rifling through the papers on his desk and was looking at her with raised eyebrows.

There was so much she wanted to say to him.

Let me live, Daddy. Let me breathe…

If only he would give her the same range he gave his musicians. At least they got to change tempo and mood. When he conducted them he made sure he breathed life into the music. He made sure it had light and shade, joy and despair, stillness and dynamism.

She had none of that freedom. She was always supposed to be the perfect little ballerina. Focused. Dedicated. Obedient. And, if her life had a score, no one would want to listen to it because it would be plodding and quiet and controlled. It would be *dull.*

'You should have told me, Daddy,' she said quietly, begging him to see past the even tone, the reasonable words. Begging him to look deep inside her and see what was longing to burst out.

He shook his head and shrugged. 'Okay,' he said dryly. 'I promise I'll tell you about the next ridiculous offer that comes along. Happy now?'

No, not really. Because this was just a symptom, wasn't it?

He shook his head again. 'Sometimes I just don't understand you, Allegra. You have the life a thousand other dancers would kill for. The life your mother dreamed about, would
have given anything to continue, and yet still it's not enough
for you. Sometimes I think I've spoiled you, and that you've
grown up a little bit selfish.'

Allegra blinked at him, stunned.

Selfish? When all she'd ever done was try to please
everyone else, try to ease their sadness by showing them
her mother had left a little bit of herself behind in her
child?

Well, the compliments were coming thick and fast today,
weren't they? First she was soulless, and now she was selfish, too. She wondered that anyone still wanted her around
if she was really that awful.

Maybe she was ungrateful and spoiled because she couldn't
stand the weight of her mother's mantle on her shoulders a
moment longer. It had been weighing her down since just
after her eighth birthday. Once she had loved feeling that her
talent had connected her to her mother, but now she wanted
that connection broken, severed once and for all.

Her mother was dead. Nothing was going to change that.

And Allegra feared that if something didn't change soon
all the life would be sucked out of her as well.

She looked at the floor and then back up at her father, giving him one last chance to really *see* her, see past layer upon
layer of expectation he'd pasted upon her, but his face was
closed. He was still angry with her. For the comment she'd
just made, for the performance last night, for the review he'd
have to defend himself against to his arty friends.

Suddenly she felt utterly and totally alone.

The only remedy was to throw herself back into her work
and hope the boiling pot of emotions she was busy trying to
keep a lid on would flow out in her next performance, and
give that critic good reason to eat his words.

'I have a rehearsal at two. I have to go.'

And, without waiting to be dismissed, she turned and left her father's study.

Nat was waiting for him at one of the airport bars. It was a pity they only had an hour or so together, otherwise they might have been able to go into Amsterdam for a meal. Finn didn't mind too much about that, though. This was the life they'd chosen and they were used to it. There'd always be another time.

He walked up to Nat and pulled her into his arms for a kiss. Nat kept her mouth firmly closed and then slid away. Finn stopped and looked at her. Same Nat, with the jaunty honey-coloured bob, the girl-next-door healthy glow about her faintly tanned skin. As usual, there was nothing girl-next-door about the clothes. They were designer all the way.

She pushed herself back onto her bar stool and took a sip of a brightly coloured cocktail with a lime-green straw and an umbrella sticking out of it. Finn frowned. Where was the usual vodka and tonic?

'What's that?' he asked, nodding towards the garish drink.

Nat's smile started in her cheeks but didn't make it all the way to her lips. 'Dutch courage, I think they call it. Want one?'

He shook his head. 'I think I'll stick to beer, thanks.' And he waved to get the bartender's attention and ordered just that.

'Finn…' Nat folded her hands in her lap and studied them for a moment, then she lifted her chin and looked him straight in the eye. 'There's no easy way to say this, so I'm just going to come out and say it.'

Finn went very still. She wasn't pregnant, was she? Because that would be *way* ahead of schedule. He was only thirty. Plenty of time for that later.

Nat inhaled. 'I've met someone,' she said quickly and re-turned her gaze to her lap.

Huh?

'Pardon?' Finn said. It was the only word he could think of.

Nat sighed and reached for her cocktail. She held the umbrella-laden glass against her chest like a shield. 'I can't marry you, Finn.'

This wasn't real. No, this definitely couldn't be real.

This wasn't Nat sitting opposite him sipping the wrong drink, saying the wrong thing. He must be having a weird in-flight dream and Schiphol airport must still be hours away.

'Who?' he said, and his voice sounded hard and flat. He couldn't look at her.

He heard her fidget in her seat. 'His name is Matthew, and he's an architect. I met him at a charity do a few months ago, and then I bumped into him a few times after that. And, well, one thing led to another...'

How he hated that phrase. It implied that something couldn't be helped, that the person in question had had no choice and, therefore, bore no responsibility.

'He's asked me to marry him,' she said quietly.

That made him whip his head round. 'But you're supposed to be marrying me!'

'I know,' Nat said, looking at him from under her lashes. 'I'm sorry.'

Finn just stared at her. He was feeling so many emotions that he wasn't even sure which one to pick out of the bag first. How about anger? A good one, that. Much better than disappointment or the sting of rejection. Or the creeping sickness telling him he'd been stupid to let himself get too attached once again.

'Sorry doesn't cut it, sweetheart! We had a deal, remember? You've got a—'

He'd been about to say *ring on your finger to prove it,* but a quick glance at her hand left him without ammunition.

Silently, she reached into her handbag, opened her purse

and handed his diamond back to him. He took it between thumb and forefinger and stared at it, felt its weight.

This *was* real.

Nat gave him a weak smile. 'We weren't really ever going to get round to it, were we, Finn? It was a nice game, pretending we were ready for a proper relationship when really we hardly spent any time together. We did it because it was easy.'

It *had* been easy! What was so wrong with that?

'We worked together, Nat! Wasn't it nice to know there was always someone to come home to? To have someone who wouldn't moan about the long hours and weeks spent apart? Someone who knew how to pick up where they left off without a lot of fuss? Is the wonderful Matthew going to put up with all of that?'

Nat sighed. 'It did work, Finn. *Did* being the operative word. "Us" was a habit we'd fallen into, a way of keeping our freedom while telling ourselves we were ready for more.'

What was she talking about? He'd been ready for more. Hadn't he? The anger quickly dissolved into confusion.

He looked at Nat and she looked back at him.

'Now I really am ready for more,' she said.

'Just not with me,' he replied, then pressed his lips into a straight line.

She shook her head. 'Matthew wants us to move to a nice big house in the country and fill it with kids.' She smiled to herself. 'I'm amazed to discover I want that, too. I'm even thinking about giving up *Amazing Planet* and doing something UK-based.'

What? Cutesy early-evening nature programmes? Nat hated those!

'But you'll go mad staying in one place for that long! You always said you didn't want to be tied down like that. This is a mistake, Nat! You love your job.'

She looked back at him, unblinking and contrite. 'I love

him more,' she said simply. 'I want to be where he is, Finn.
I can't stand being away from him.'

Finn slumped back into his leather-backed stool. She was
crazy, but there was no talking to her. She'd made her choice
and, even if she regretted it later, he wasn't going to stop her.
And he certainly wasn't going to beg. So it was time to cut
ties, to let her loose, he supposed.

They sat in silence for a couple of minutes, watching the
crowds bustle past. Families with whining kids and stupid
big Spanish hats that no one born there would disgrace themselves by wearing. Elderly couples on city breaks who'd probably seen Amsterdam's canals from the wrong side of a coach
window.

He turned away, irritated, and found Nat watching him.

'That was us, Finn. We were tourists.'

Finn glanced at the almost-empty cocktail glass. What *exactly* was in that concoction? Nat knew he'd never been on
a package holiday in his life, knew he'd rather shoot himself
first.

She stood up, looking very serious. 'I want the real experience now, Finn. I don't want to just whizz past the land-
marks—dating, engagement, wedding—and still not really
know what it's like to live there.'

That drink had really gone to her head. She wasn't making any sense at all.

'I hate to ask, but would you do me a favour? Will you
keep quiet about this until I get back from Tonga next week?
I don't want media speculation running rife while we're both
out of the country.'

He nodded. She could have anything she wanted. He didn't
care. He was numb. Just as well, really, because he was in no
hurry to find out what a broken heart felt like.

She leaned forward and pressed a soft kiss to his cheek.
'Goodbye, Finn. I hope you find what you're looking for.'

And then she was gone. Lost amongst the overladen trolleys and duty free bags.

The bartender plonked his bottle of beer in front of him and Finn took a long, long drink.

Jilted in the time it took to order a beer. Marvellous.

'I want to see that lift again.'

Allegra picked herself up off the studio floor and glared at her partner. Damien, *The Little Mermaid*'s choreographer, continued to stare at them, his patience thinning rapidly.

So was Allegra's.

'It would help if you put your hands where they're supposed to go,' she muttered darkly to Stephen. He was in a particularly infantile mood this afternoon.

Stephen helped her up, spun her into his arms and proceeded to take hold of her a good few inches *south* of where he was supposed to. Allegra clenched her teeth, prised his hand from her left buttock and moved it to her hip.

'You're no fun any more,' Stephen moaned, not in the least bit repentant.

She placed one hand on his shoulder, the other on his cheek and got into position. 'You and I have never had that kind of fun, Stephen, and nor are we likely to,' she said, as she tipped her head to the correct angle.

Pity, that. Because Stephen was blond and finely sculpted, and just about the only man under fifty she saw on a regular basis who wasn't gay. But Stephen had the morals of an alley cat, and made the most of being a good-looking straight male in a predominantly female profession. When it came to women, flirting was Stephen's default position. However, as long as any physical contact between them was strictly professional, Stephen was pretty harmless. Most of the time she ignored it and they got along fine, but this afternoon she really needed to impress Damien and her partner was not making it easy.

'I think there are a few of the corps that you haven't slept with lurking in the corridors hoping to catch a glimpse of you. Why don't you see if you can rid them of their girlish illusions once rehearsal's over and leave me alone?'

'Careful, darling,' he said as he dipped her backwards and then lifted her into the air. 'Or soon they'll be calling you the Little Cactus instead of the Little Mermaid.'

The rehearsal went fine after that. At least, Allegra had thought it was going fine. She lost herself in the dancing, just as she'd done in the early days, and forgot about everything— the reviews, her father, even the telephone call that had made her heart soar, just for a moment. Instead she concentrated on bones and joints and muscles, on shapes and lines and angles. It was a blessed relief.

'No, no, no!' Damien shouted as they got to the end of a particularly difficult combination. The pianist who'd been accompanying them broke off mid-bar.

'You're supposed to be the picture of innocent longing, my dear,' the choreographer said, turning away from her and running his hand through his hair. 'Do try and put some feeling into it or the audience will be dropping off to sleep.' He turned to the pianist. 'From the top—again.'

So they did it again. And again.

Allegra looked deep inside herself, pulled out everything she could find in there—and there was quite a shopping list, she discovered. Grief for a lost parent and a lost childhood. Resentment for every person who'd pushed and pulled and ordered her around in the last decade. And, yes, longing too. Longing for a pair of deep brown eyes and a crinkly smile, for a life of adventure that could never be hers. She poured it all in there and when they'd finished that section she was drained.

She broke away from Stephen and headed for her water bottle on the floor near the mirrors, then she picked up her towel and wiped the sweat off her face, neck and shoulders.

She turned to find Damien surveying her with hard eyes.

'I can see you're trying, Allegra, but it's not enough. I need more.' He nodded to the pianist. 'From the start of the adagio...'

Allegra walked over to Stephen, a slight twinge in her right ankle making her favour the other foot, and they assumed the starting position for their pas de deux. The pianist pounded the keys and Allegra closed her eyes, told her exhausted body it could do this and started to move.

After no more than ten bars of music Damien interrupted them. 'More, Allegra! I need more!' he yelled as she turned and jumped, spun and balanced.

'More!' he shouted as Stephen propelled her into the air, turned her upside down and then swung her back to the ground.

Damien stamped his foot in time to the music, driving them on through the final and most physically demanding section. *'More!'*

I don't have anything more to give, Allegra thought, her body on the verge of collapse. *Surely this has to be enough.*

The music ended and she and Stephen slid apart and sank to the floor, panting. The choreographer marched over and stood towering above them. Allegra looked up.

'Not good enough, Allegra. I don't know what's wrong with you, but you'd better buck your ideas up by tomorrow's rehearsal or I'll replace you and Stephen in Saturday's performance with Tamzin and Valeri. I will not have months of my hard work undone by one lukewarm ballerina. Now get out of my rehearsal and don't come back until you're truly prepared to commit to this role!'

His face was pink now. Allegra was speechless. She looked at the clock. They still had half an hour. He couldn't really be—

'Get out,' Damien said, and pointed to the door.

So Allegra left. She quickly changed her shoes and pulled

on her stretchy black trousers, then she picked up her things, pushed the studio door open with her hip and walked out.

And she kept on walking. Out of the rehearsal studio, out of the building and out of her life.

CHAPTER FOUR

ALLEGRA'S brain was swimming. She'd just jumped out of a helicopter and *onto* Finn McLeod! And now he was standing over her, grinning like a maniac while the wind whipped around them, offering his hand.

She took it. How could she have done anything else?

She couldn't tell if this was better or worse than her late-night fantasies when she'd been stuck on an island with no one but Fearless Finn for company—and entertainment. A big blob of water fell out of the sky and crashed onto her scalp, but Allegra was only aware of it in a distant, out-of-body kind of way.

The awareness that came from the warm hand clasped around her own? Now that was very much up-close and immediate, and definitely, definitely *in* her body. Just that simple action had caused her flesh to tingle and her pulse to do a series of jetés.

She was touching Finn McLeod. Actually holding his hand.

And as she looked into his eyes once again she realised that while TV Finn was just plain gorgeous, In The Flesh Finn had the kind of presence that made a girl's nerve endings sizzle and her eyes water.

Or could that have something to do with the rain?

To be honest, she didn't really care. She didn't care about anything now; she was a million miles away from her life and *Finn McLeod* was holding her hand and talking to her in that beautiful Scottish accent of his. All she wanted to do was stare into those impossibly deep brown eyes…

Oh.

He'd been talking.

And now he'd stopped. He was also frowning at her. Why?

She suddenly became aware of the tension in his arm muscles, of the tugging sensation in her shoulder socket. He was pulling her. She was supposed to moving, getting up. Not letting her behind get damp on the sand. Not gawping at the most gorgeous-looking man she'd ever seen in real life.

Thankfully, she was well used to telling her body to do things it had no real inclination to do. She issued a command to her feet and legs and they obligingly pushed down into the sand, levering her upwards with the help of Finn's hand, until she was standing opposite him.

Nobody moved for a few seconds. Not even the guy with the camera.

She'd done what he'd wanted, hadn't she? She'd stood up. So why was he staring at her as if he wasn't sure if she was human or not?

The downside to not being able to tear her gaze away from the deep brown eyes was that she was now privy to the slide-show of emotions flashing through them.

Bewilderment. Concern. Uncertainty.

And since he hadn't looked anywhere else but right back at her since she'd sent him crashing onto the moist sand, the only conclusion she could come to was that he must be feeling all of those things about *her*.

Not good, Allegra. Pull yourself together. You know how to do that, don't you? You should do. Part of the training. It should come as naturally as the other basics, like pliés and tendus.

She wrenched her gaze from his and stared out to sea, fixed it on the retreating black blob of the helicopter flying low over the water. It was much farther away than she'd thought it would be. Just how long *had* she been sitting on the beach, staring into Finn's eyes?

'Okay,' she heard Finn say. 'We'd better start sorting out some kind of shelter before it gets dark, or tonight will be our most miserable on the planet.'

She turned to face the land and watched him as he trudged up the beach towards the dense green vegetation fringing its edge. The camera guy, however, didn't move. He just kept pointing his lens at Allegra, his feet braced into the sand.

She'd forgotten about the unseen bodies behind the camera when she'd phoned Finn's producer back and agreed to do this. When the show aired it often seemed as if Finn was totally alone in whatever strange and exotic world he was exploring. And that was what she'd latched onto when she'd marched out of the rehearsal studio and had dug for her phone in her pocket—the chance of her very own private adventure with Fearless Finn.

Another drop of rain hit her scalp, as fat as a water bomb. She stared back at the camera lens, doing nothing, saying nothing. Just what exactly had she got herself into?

'Come on, Dave,' Finn yelled from under a huge palm tree as the water bombs began to multiply. Allegra couldn't be sure, but it seemed as if someone up there was aiming them directly at her, and they were an awfully good shot. Her long-sleeved shirt only had a few dry patches on it now, and water was dripping from her shorts down her bare legs.

Dave merely adjusted the focus ring on his camera, keeping it pointed straight at Allegra. 'Not my job, mate!' he yelled back. 'I'm here to capture you two battling to survive the elements.'

She narrowed her eyes at the beady lens still trained on her, then took off up the beach, following her secret crush. If she stood next to Finn, that contraption would have to focus on something other than just her.

The camera—and Dave—followed.

'You can look smug all you want,' said Finn to his colleague, 'but this storm is picking up fast and I doubt they'll be sending the speedboat to pick you up and take you back to the hotel anytime soon.' He bestowed a crinkly-eyed grin on Dave that made Allegra want to sit back down on the damp sand again. It was the hint of determination behind the laughter in his eyes that did it. The soft hairs behind her ears stood on end.

'I reckon you've got two choices,' Finn added. 'Either you put that thing down and help us build a shelter big enough for three, or you can get all the footage you want, and when we've finished making our two-man lean-to we'll make sure you get some great shots of us waving to you from the warm and dry.'

Fair choice, Allegra thought. Dave might not like it, but at least he had an option.

Dave grunted and pulled his camera off his shoulder. 'I need to get the rain cover on, anyway,' he muttered. 'But I'm going to have to film some of the time—or Simon will have my hide.'

'And a lovely rug for his office you'd make, too,' Finn said, then pulled an absolutely huge knife from somewhere on his person and marched over to a clump of bamboo poles almost as thick as Allegra's arms and began hacking at the base of one of them.

In no time at all he'd felled a good few. She stood there, watching him. It was odd, this sensation of being totally superfluous. Normally when she was at work everything revolved around her. She hadn't realised how much she'd taken that for granted—or how much she'd actually liked it.

It was as if he'd totally forgotten she was there.

She coughed.

Finn hacked at bamboo.

She coughed again. 'Is there anything I can do?'

Finn's head snapped round, and she realised that her existence had indeed slipped his mind. He turned back to the bamboo before answering. 'Yes. Go and collect some palm leaves and split them down the middle.' And then he reached into a little pocket on his trousers, pulled out a small folding knife and tossed it onto the ground behind him.

Allegra reached forward and picked it up. She eased it open and stared at it.

She didn't think she'd ever held anything like this before in her life. No need for tools like this in the cultured and contained garden squares of Notting Hill. She didn't even know how to open it without cutting herself.

She almost opened her mouth to say as much, but then thought better of it.

She'd wanted something different, hadn't she? No point complaining that 'different' was much less comfortable than she'd thought it would be. She just hadn't expected to feel quite so much like a fish out of water.

The knife lay glinting in her hand.

Palm leaves? She looked around. Well, no shortage of them nearby, it seemed. It didn't take more than ten minutes for her to gather a whole armful of such material. She dragged them back to where Finn was finishing with the bamboo and dumped them in a pile on the ground.

Finn rose from sitting on his haunches and put his hands on his hips as he scanned the area, looking for heaven knew what. She hoped it wasn't snakes. But it didn't matter what he was looking for or what he asked her to do. She'd seen every episode of his show and she knew he could look after himself in this jungle. And her. As a result, if Finn McLeod asked her to stand on her head and sing *Twinkle, Twinkle,* she'd do it. No questions asked.

So when Finn asked her to clear a patch of ground with a stick, she cleared a patch of ground with a stick, and she didn't think about snakes. And when he showed her how to make rope out of vines and creepers, she plaited until her fingers were sore and numb with cold.

Meanwhile, Finn and Dave rigged up a simple triangular structure by lashing the bamboo poles together with her lumpily woven twine. It had a raised platform and a sloping roof frame that rose high at the front and joined the base at the back. Once it was steady enough, they blinked against the rain and worked on thatching the roof with the leaves she'd collected.

It was dry inside. *Warm* might have been stretching it a little.

They climbed inside, all three of them soaked to the skin, and sat in silence watching the water tip from the sky in skip loads.

You couldn't call it rain. Rain didn't blur the vision and make the sea boil. Rain was that delicate grey drizzle on a November afternoon in London. Or the short-lived exuberance of an April shower. This water falling from the sky with such weight and ferocity deserved another name entirely.

It might have been *just* bearable if she'd been sitting next to Finn, but Dave had barged his way between them when they'd climbed in, and she could hardly even see Finn past the cameraman's muscular bulk.

'Don't suppose you could build a fire, could you?' Dave asked hopefully.

'Too wet,' Finn replied. 'We'll have to wait for a break in the weather.'

Dave humphed. 'Thought Fearless Finn's motto was "Expect the impossible!"'

Finn just grinned back at him, then leaned forward to look at the sky again. 'Just as well it isn't rainy season,' he said quite seriously.

Allegra was tempted to laugh. Really throw her head back and howl.

She didn't, of course.

Instead she shifted from one buttock to the other. The only thing between her and the ground was a floor of hard bamboo poles. Finn had said they'd make it more comfortable with leaves and moss when there was dry foliage to be found, but until then it was bamboo or nothing. However, Allegra had very little in the way of padding on her derrière to make the former an attractive proposition.

Finn looked back at the pair of them, huddled nearer the back of the shelter. 'Don't think this is going to let off while it's still light, though.' He slapped Dave sympathetically on the shoulder. 'You're definitely stuck with us for the night.'

The hulk sitting next to her grunted again.

Hang on.

What had Finn said earlier?

'D-did...'

Oh, bother. Her teeth were chattering. She clenched her jaw shut in an effort to still them, then tried again.

'Did y-you say something about a hotel?'

Finn sighed. He had that bewildered-concerned-uncertain look on his face again. 'Don't believe all that internet chatter about me staying in five-star hotels and pretending I'm roughing it. On *Fearless Finn,* it's the real deal.'

She'd said something wrong, hadn't she? She looked at Dave. She was *sure* that Finn had said something about a hotel. Surely, they did something like that in emergencies? At times like this?

Finn caught her looking at Dave and read her mind. 'Only the crew get that luxury. Dave needs to go back to base every evening to charge his batteries, get fresh tapes and to deliver the footage so Simon can watch the rushes. At night it *should* just be you, me, a night-vision camera rigged to a tree and a hand-held for us to use in case anything interesting happens.

Allegra felt her shoulders sag.

If that wasn't bad enough news, she had a sneaking suspicion that her version of *interesting* when she and Finn were left here alone might be vastly different from his.

Just at that moment a crack of thunder split the sky above their heads, accompanied by a flash of lightning that seemed to arc from one edge of the horizon to the other. Allegra jumped so high she rattled the shelter. If it were possible, it began to rain even harder.

Finn stayed crouching at the front of the shelter, peering into the darkening chaos outside with a strange light in his eyes.

'Isn't it amazing?' he asked, unable to tear his gaze away from the meteorological light show that was shaking the ground and rattling the very heavens.

'Bloody fabulous,' said Dave in a weary voice and flopped backward to sprawl on the bamboo poles.

Allegra really wanted to *want* to join Finn at the edge of the shelter, to mirror back to him the strange sense of awe in his eyes, but her bones felt so cold and damp she was sure they'd locked into position. So she didn't do anything but sit huddled in a ball while the bamboo left permanent dents in her bottom, and tried to ignore the feeling she'd just made the worst mistake of her life.

The thunder was easing now, much to Finn's disappointment. The rain continued, however. *That* he could have lived without. He and his two companions were still mighty damp, and there'd be no hope of drying out fully until the sun came up or he managed to build a fire. From the taste of the air, the smell of the bulbous clouds still dropping their loads, he'd guess the possibility was still hours away. That was a long time to wait with an out-of-sorts camera operator and a mouse-like ballerina.

Thinking of the ballerina... Night had fallen while the storm had been raging and she didn't have much in the way of body fat to keep her warm. Dave, meanwhile, had more than enough. She'd be better off between the two of them.

'Hey, Dave,' he called into the darkness. 'Why don't you swap places with—' what was her name again? '—Allegra?'

There was a short silence and then Dave sighed. The shelter shook, there was a whole lot of shuffling noises, an outraged female gasp followed by a mumbled apology, and then a reluctant Dave-type chuckle.

'Just as well Anya Pirelli pulled out last minute,' he muttered. 'My missus would have confiscated certain parts of my anatomy and fried them up for breakfast if that had just happened with her.'

The taut little figure who was now beside Finn stiffened further and he winced on her behalf.

It wasn't that she wasn't feminine or attractive in her own understated, lean way. It was just that she wasn't...well, Anya Pirelli. And there was nothing that she, or the other three billion women on the planet, could do about it.

'I'm surprised Nat let you sign old Anya up in the first place,' Dave added, snorting dryly.

A quiet voice murmured beside him in the blackness, almost as if she was speaking to herself and hadn't meant to be overheard. 'Nat?'

'His fiancée,' Dave said matter-of-factly. 'Been engaged a while now. Took his time asking her, though. How long was it you'd been together? Three years? Four?'

The completeness of the tropical night meant he didn't see the hearty slap Dave delivered to his shoulder coming.

'Five,' Finn said, noticing the defensive tone in his voice with no visuals to distract him. He really didn't want to get into this right now. Having to build a shelter in the pouring rain had been a lovely distraction from the gaping chasm that had recently opened up in his personal life, thank you very much. And what business of Dave's was it, anyway?

He shouldn't be bothered by it, but people like Dave didn't

realise that he and Nat hadn't had a traditional relationship. Their work schedules had meant they'd been apart more than they'd been together in five years, so it had been closer to one and a half years in normal people's terms.

Dave sighed, his voice still tinged with good humour. 'Didn't think there was a woman alive who'd make old Finn here settle down!'

'I'm not *settling* anywhere,' Finn said quickly. And then he remembered his promise to Nat to keep quiet about the split and decided not to elaborate further. *Settling down...* Ugh. He hated that phrase, and probably would have reacted to it anyway. 'I just felt I'd reached an age when it was time to stop wandering around and put down some roots.'

Nat's comments from the previous evening started to swirl around his head, but he batted them away as if they were mosquitoes.

There was a mournful little sound from the huddled figure beside him. It started off almost like a moan but ended like a yawn. She must be exhausted. He and Dave were used to this relentless schedule, but it was hard on their guests. There wasn't much to do now but wait until the rain stopped and talk amongst themselves, but Dave was as subtle—and as discreet—as a foghorn, and the sooner they ended this topic of conversation the better.

'We might as well try to get some rest,' Finn said.

All three of them shuffled until they were lying on the bamboo floor of the shelter. Finn was instantly still, but the other two fidgeted for quite some time. Hardly surprising, on a bed like this. Eventually, though, everything went still and quiet.

They weren't quite touching, but he could sense Allegra was as stiff horizontal as she had been vertical. How odd. He was sure her name was more familiar now he thought about it, that Nat had dragged him along to watch her perform when they'd first been seeing each other.

Allegra Martin. That was her name.

He tried to sharpen the brief, fuzzy snatches of memory from that night. There wasn't much to go on. He couldn't remember where he and Nat had gone for dinner before the performance, or what either of them had worn, or even if they'd gone home together afterwards, but he remembered Allegra's dancing.

Despite the fact he'd moaned loud and long about being dragged to Covent Garden, he'd actually been struck by the unexpected beauty of it all. Odd, really. Because to Finn McLeod beauty wasn't normally found caged within four walls and a ceiling, no matter how grand the old building was. True beauty was usually found in wild, open spaces.

She must have been really young then. Little more than a kid. And yet he'd never seen something move that way before—so free and fluid and graceful. Except maybe the Northern Lights over the Arctic.

Didn't seem to have much of that fluidity about her now, though, which was a pity. In the wild, you had to go with the flow. She was going to need every bit of flexibility she possessed if she was going to survive the challenges of the coming week.

He sighed, folded his hands behind his head and peered up into the featureless sky, hoping to see the twinkle of a star eventually. Perhaps conversation would have been better, because now the other two castaways were asleep he was left alone with his thoughts.

He'd thought he and Nat were the perfect couple. What on earth had gone wrong? He just didn't get it.

Must still be numb, though, because he wasn't feeling half as crushed as he'd expected to. Sad and disappointed, yes, but not devastated. But that was because he was strong, he supposed. Resilient.

He thought he saw a pinprick of light up above and stilled his thoughts for a few seconds while he tried to focus on it.

Hmm. Having a broken heart wasn't nearly as bad as people said it was. He'd always thought those people who sang the whiny love ballads on the radio were being overly dramatic, and now he felt justifiably superior about being right about it all along.

He had a feeling his heart was mending already. In true *Fearless Finn* style, he was sure he'd survive.

The drip of water on the leaves above her head was keeping Allegra awake. At least, that was what she was telling herself. Drips and the cold. And the ridges of the bamboo poles, of course. It certainly wasn't anything else.

Not the sense of being turned upside down and back to front. Not the electric charge thrumming between her and the man lying next to her. Or the fact it was almost certainly a one-way sensation. No, those things weren't bothering her at all.

She sighed and rolled over onto her back. Every part of the motion was painful. She'd be bruised from head to toe in the morning, wouldn't be able to dance properly for days...

Her stomach dropped to the same chilly temperature as the night air swirling around inside their makeshift shelter.

Dancing.

She wasn't planning on doing any of that for the next seven days, was she? So it really shouldn't matter. She wouldn't be there to dance the Saturday evening performance of *The Little Mermaid.* Tamzin would be thrilled to take her place. So there was no need for Allegra to rehearse, no need to do class.

She sat up and hugged her arms around herself. Everyone would be furious with her. Stephen. Her father. The choreographer. The Artistic Director of the company... The list was endless.

She'd let them all down.

Guilt washed over her, matching its tempo to the crash of

surf on the beach. She hugged herself tighter and rested her chin on her knees.

But she'd been letting them all down for months, anyway, hadn't she? Who wanted a soulless robot as their partner, or their principal dancer? Or their daughter?

And now she was seeing the same hesitation in the eyes of the one man she'd hoped would save her from it. *Collecting leaves and plaiting vines?* He didn't think she could do it, did he? Didn't think she'd last a week on this island. She swivelled her head to look at Finn. Couldn't see him, though, even though his feet must be right beside her. It was way too dark. She wanted very badly to poke him in the ribs right now and tell him he was wrong.

She didn't, of course.

Mostly because she feared he was right. Escaping from her life had been such a wonderful fantasy. But that was all it had ever been—a fantasy. Too bad she hadn't realised that before she'd snapped and turned it into a reality.

Now she was stuck here on a stormy desert island with a surly cameraman capturing her every shortcoming and a man who saw what everyone else saw when they looked at her. A disappointment.

To make matters worse, she'd probably kissed goodbye to her career as well. What *had* she been thinking?

Nothing.

She hadn't been thinking at all, simply reacting. Like a tectonic plate that after years of crushing pressure had popped free, sending tremors in all directions. Every area of her life had been affected by this one rash decision. The only rash decision she'd ever made. She should have been thankful for her stale little life. At least last week she'd *had* a life.

Finn shifted position beside her and her heart did a little skip, a little flutter, and then settled back into place. She eased herself back down gently so she was facing him in the darkness, could feel the warmth of his even breath on her cheek.

The rain was easing off now, but she didn't really register it because the drumming of her pulse in her ears picked up the insistent rhythm and kept it going.

This was stupid. She was reacting to his every movement, his every breath, as if she really *were* a love-struck teenager. At least, she imagined this was how teenage crushes went. She hadn't really had time for them when she'd been the right age.

She'd lost herself in dancing in her teenage years—her way of coping with her mother's death. When she'd been dancing, she hadn't had to think about anything else. She'd been able to shelve the grief and let other emotions flow through her instead. Such a relief. But at some point in the last decade that well had dried up. She couldn't seem to feel anything any more. She'd even stopped missing her mother.

Soulless...

She closed her eyes against the velvet darkness, even though it made no difference—shut out no extra light from her eyeballs.

In the utter and complete darkness senses other than sight started working overtime. Her whole body throbbed in response to the nearness of Finn. It seemed those set-aside teenage hormones had definitely caught up with her. She'd not really had many chances to release them before now. She'd had a few relationships, all brief and fairly unsatisfying, all eventually sacrificed to a career that didn't believe in evenings and weekends.

And then one night after a performance, when she'd been too hyped up to sleep, she'd switched on the television and clapped eyes on Finn McLeod, and that had been that.

Teenage crush. Big time.

Except most teenagers didn't get the opportunity to do anything but stare at a poster on their bedroom wall. If they were lucky, they might catch a fleeting glimpse of their crush outside a theatre or a TV studio. They certainly weren't offered the chance to spend a week alone with him on a desert island.

And there lay the problem.

Crush and opportunity had collided, and now she was reaping the consequences. Unfortunately, sleep was nowhere to be found and in the silence and darkness consequences were hitting her fast and hard in the middle of her forehead.

She breathed out slowly and lay very still.

She'd done it now. There was no going back. She'd have to live with those consequences. Even the fact that Finn McLeod thought she was a hopeless substitute for the hot tennis player who should have been lying beside him in the shelter instead of her.

In the midst of all the doubts and fears swirling inside her, something happened. Something small hardened. A tiny seed. A kernel of determination and perseverance. The very thing that had helped her survive ballet school and the early days of the company and had rocketed her to where she was now.

She'd show him. She'd ace every task, follow every instruction to the letter.

Come morning, she'd show Finn McLeod—and the surly cameraman—exactly what she was made of.

CHAPTER FIVE

A NOISE startled Allegra from a shallow sleep. She'd been dreaming of being made to walk a tightrope over a deep, dark chasm, only the tightrope had morphed into an endless succession of bamboo poles. Somewhere below her she'd heard Finn McLeod, urging her to jump, telling her he'd catch her, but he'd been hidden in the darkness. She'd had no idea where he was or how far down she'd have to fall before he saved her, so she'd just kept walking the bamboo poles until her feet had throbbed and her soles had bled.

She sat up quickly—too quickly—to rub her feet and check they were okay, but the unexpected discovery of a heavy hiking boot where she'd expected to find tender flesh meant she jammed one finger backwards in an awkward direction and had to stifle a yelp of pain.

She shook her head and rubbed her eyes. Those boots made her feet feel like foreign objects. Heavy and dull and stiff. None of the clothes she was wearing—bar her underwear—were her own. Not the cargo trousers stuffed into her backpack or the shorts, vest top and beige long-sleeved shirt she was wearing now. The decision to come had been so last-minute and she'd had nothing remotely suitable in her wardrobe, so the production company had kitted her out. Sparsely.

Consciousness returned enough for her to glance around and orient herself—not that she had totally forgotten where she was. The poles beneath her were a too-constant reminder for that.

She was alone in the shelter, and outside it was light. Not *too* bright, but definitely light. Carefully, very carefully, she bottom-shuffled her way to the edge of the shelter and peered out.

Oh, wow.

This morning the beach looked a totally different place. The sand that had seemed a dirty beige yesterday was now a shimmering pale gold, and the churning grey sky had melted into the soft blue of a baby's blanket. She was still cold, though. They'd made their camp at the fringes of the jungle, where sand and earth met, and the long shapes of the trees reaching down the beach meant the shelter was still shrouded in shadow.

Her legs were as stiff as if she'd done three performances of *Swan Lake* back to back, and they creaked as she swung them over the edge of the shelter's sleeping platform and let the weight of her boots pull her feet downwards onto the sandy earth.

She stretched a little—an unbreakable habit from her train-ing—stood up and walked away from the shelter, further down the beach, wondering where her fellow castaways were. There were footprints in the sand leading off to the right and then curving towards the jungle, but none coming back the same way.

She was completely on her own. Nobody to tell her how to behave or think or even move. There was a whole beach of virgin sand, swept clean by the morning's tide, waiting for her. She could lie down and make sand angels if she wanted, or cartwheel down to the shore and plop into the sea.

She didn't, of course.

After staring at the vast expanse for a few seconds, she turned and followed the footprints, placing her feet carefully inside the larger dents in the sand.

She hadn't paid too much attention to her home for the coming week the evening before. Too busy trying to get the shelter up to worry about the scenery. Their camp was on a wide strip of sand that filled almost all of a gently curving bay with low rocky headlands at either end. At the left edge of the bay, maybe only thirty feet out to sea, was a small island. Well, a large rock, really. But its top must have been above the high tide line because a small tree grew on top, giving just enough shade for some scrubby grass to flourish underneath.

Away from the shore, the land was covered with dense green vegetation, and rose gently until it peaked in a rocky hill. Not exactly mountainous, but with the lack of any other geographical features, it seemed enormous.

It struck her that she didn't even properly know where she was—except the surf on the beach was the Pacific and the nearest land mass was Panama.

She stopped walking and turned on the spot. Where had Finn and the cameraman got to?

Even though the rising sun was now starting to warm her face she shivered. Her clothes were still damp from the night before and her stomach was very, very empty. It was beautiful here, to be sure, but she had a sudden overwhelming sense of her own vulnerability.

She was saved from pondering a slow and nasty death from starvation by a crashing sound. She'd reached the end of the tracks in the sand now, where they disappeared into the undergrowth, and before she could decide whether she should freeze or run, Finn burst through the bushes and was standing before her, dragging what looked like half a dead tree behind him. Dave appeared a few seconds later, puffing and muttering things under his breath that she was glad she couldn't hear.

'Great! You're up,' Finn said, and smiled at her.

She nodded, suddenly unsure of what to say. The whole of

the English language was at her disposal. All she had to do was pick a word. And what did she do? She nodded. Pathetic. But there were too many words. There was too much choice, and faced with so many overwhelming options she'd backed away and chosen nothing.

'First things first,' Finn said, marching back towards the camp, obliterating his own footprints as he went. 'We need to build a fire and get warm, and we need to worry about food and water.'

Worry? Allegra almost laughed out loud. When did Fearless Finn worry about anything? He seemed to be glowing with strength and health and confidence this morning, as if the night battling the elements had revitalised him somehow.

She sighed and scurried after him.

No wonder the TV cameras ate him up. No wonder a whole army of women back home had linked themselves on the internet through blogs and social networking sites and referred to themselves as 'Finn's Fanatics'.

But the camera didn't catch all of him. It didn't catch the raw energy that pulsed from every pore, the sense that anything and everything could and *would* happen around him, even—as the show's tagline hinted—the impossible. It definitely didn't catch the way his throwaway smiles turned a girl's knees to chocolate.

Allegra flicked a look across at Dave. While she'd been admiring the rear view of Finn dragging the tree across the beach, he'd trained the camera back on her.

She wanted to growl. Instead she swallowed.

Cameras might not catch all of Finn, but she knew they were very good at catching all sorts of things that people didn't think they'd given away, and the last thing she wanted was the camera noticing *her* noticing Finn. That would be far, far too humiliating.

* * *

Finn watched carefully as Allegra struck his knife on the flint he'd given her. Not even a spark. And there wasn't likely to be one if she kept *stroking* that knife against the flint. The fluffed up coconut husk underneath would never catch light. It was her first go at something like this, though—that much was obvious—so he bit his tongue and sat back on his haunches and watched. For now. She'd get it eventually; she just needed to find her own rhythm with it.

Far from moaning about being cold and damp this morning, she'd hardly said a word. She'd just stared at him with her doll's eyes, listening intently to every word that had dropped out of his mouth about tinder and kindling and fuel, and then she'd helped him gather exactly the right stuff, no further guidance necessary. And when he'd explained how to build the fire, she'd watched and then reproduced, following his instructions to the letter.

Far from being a diva, this little ballerina was turning out to be a pleasant surprise.

The only thing lacking now was a spark.

She paused her efforts and glanced up at him, a questioning, slightly panic-laced expression in her eyes. It was the first time that morning he'd seen her show any emotion at all.

'In the wild places of this planet, fire is everything,' he said quietly, and her eyes grew the tiniest bit wider and rounder. 'Without fire, we couldn't survive. We need it to purify the water, to cook, to provide protection and warmth. I'll give you plenty more opportunities to learn, but for now I think we're cold enough for me to take over.'

She blinked and her chin rose an almost imperceptible amount.

Finn let a half-smile pull one side of his mouth upwards. A little bit stubborn, too, this girl. Good. She'd need that if she was going to pass the challenges this week would bring—especially the final surprise challenge he put all his celebrity guests through in the new programme format.

She handed the knife and flint over to him and he set about starting the fire.

'Actually, there's one thing that's even more important than fire in survival situations,' he said.

The coconut husk was smoking now. He picked the ball of fluff up and blew on it gently, coaxing the flame to life. Making a fire took practice, but it also took instinct—knowing exactly the right time to trust the almost invisible sparks to do their job, when to blow, how hard and for how long.

A tiny orange flame sprang from almost nowhere, and he turned the ball of fibres in his hand, letting it grow, and then he placed it gently on the fire pit they'd created and starting stacking the kindling around it. He couldn't help himself; he had to smile. He always got a kick out of this, no matter how many times he did it. He glanced up at Allegra and found her smiling back at him.

At least, he *thought* that was Allegra. The soft, barely-there smile completely transformed her, lighting up her face more than the growing flames could have done.

Ouch.

He dropped the twig he'd been holding and sucked at his fingers. The flickering heat had got a little too close for comfort. That didn't happen very often any more. He obviously hadn't been paying proper attention. Time to get back to the subject in hand.

'More than anything—more than survival skills, plant knowledge, physical strength or navigational ability—the thing that keeps us alive out here where mankind doesn't normally dwell is *spark.*'

'Spark?' she said, lines in her forehead banishing the curve in her mouth. 'Isn't that the same as fire?'

He shook his head as he shuffled back and reached for some larger branches and put them on the fire. 'No. I mean the spark *inside.* That something…that flicker of human spirit that keeps us from giving in, that keeps us struggling for the next breath. If you've got that, you can survive against the odds, even if you are stuck in alien territory.' He shrugged one shoulder. 'The survival training makes it easier, but with *spark* nothing is impossible.'

She nodded, but she didn't look very happy about what he'd said. In fact, that eager, open look she'd been wearing since they'd crouched down to build the fire disappeared.

'You mean something like *soul?*' she said quietly, her eyes fixed on his face.

'That's it.'

She looked at the sandy earth beneath their feet. And then she stood up and walked a few paces further down the beach and looked out to sea. Her arms came around her front and she hugged her elbows tightly.

Hmm. Maybe this compliant-seeming woman had more of the touch of the diva about her than he'd first imagined. He shrugged to himself and chucked another log on the now roaring fire. He wasn't pandering to it, though. She'd have to learn *that* quick-smart as well.

'The next important thing to do is to get dry,' he said over his shoulder. And then, just because he couldn't resist, 'It's a real morale booster.'

She twisted her neck to look back at him, and then she turned and walked up to the blaze, extending her arms until they were rigid and flexing her palms back.

Finn gave a chuckle. 'You'll spend all day trying to dry those clothes like that.' And then, as the little ballerina's eyes grew the roundest and bluest he'd ever seen them, he began to strip off.

Well, it seemed her prophecy that anything could and would happen when Finn McLeod was around hadn't been far off the mark. Allegra wasn't sure whether to pull up a metaphorical chair and enjoy herself, or slink off into the shelter to protect them both from embarrassment.

A low, rumbling snort from behind her caused her to yank her head round. Dave was finding it all highly amusing as he caught every millisecond of her double-edged reaction with his big zoom lens. Oh, how she was learning to hate that object!

She turned her back on both man and camera. However, this meant the only other view open to her was Finn and his rapidly diminishing wardrobe. His shirt was already on the ground, revealing a broad and rather finely muscled back, and he had turned his attention to his boot laces. Allegra swallowed. After that the only items left would be his trousers and his—she gulped again—underwear.

She stood frozen to the spot, unable to move, unable to look away.

Why was she reacting like this? It wasn't as if she hadn't seen her fair share of unadorned male bodies in her line of work. And she'd certainly watched enough episodes of *Fearless Finn* to know that he had no compunction about getting naked if the situation called for it, but there had always been a little bit of post-production wizardry that had fuzzied out the...um...*essentials.* She suddenly missed that fuzzy square very much indeed.

Finn was out of his boots now and had pulled his trousers down to his knees. The sight of his thighs made Allegra's mouth go dry.

He paused and looked up at her. 'Come on, then.' His cheeky grin turned her already parched tongue to sandpaper. 'You'll go mouldy if you stay in those damp things.'

He stepped out of his cargo trousers and picked them up, along with his shirt, and then hung them out on one of the large bushes that circled their camp, making sure they were stretched out wide and facing the roaring fire.

Her heart rate began to slow a little. He was stopping at his underwear—at least that was how it looked for now. Part of her was relieved, but the other part? Well, it just...wasn't.

Once Finn had finished arranging his clothes on the bush he turned back to her. She discovered she was clutching at the front of her light cotton shirt, pulling the edges towards each other, even though it was still buttoned up.

What must she look like?

A timid child? A complete prude? Certainly nothing like the kind of impulsive, free-spirited woman who would appeal to Finn McLeod. The kind of girl who would smile back at the gorgeous hunk of man who had nonchalantly got half-naked beside her and was inviting her to do the same. The kind of girl who already *had* claimed his heart, she reminded herself.

Finn jerked his head towards the sparkling pale green shallows. 'I'm going to wash off the helicopter, the storm and anything else that might be clinging to me,' he said. And then he bounded off down the sand and threw himself into the surf.

Well, she couldn't stand here getting damper and sweatier and smellier by the second, could she? If there was one thing she wanted—besides Finn McLeod—it was to feel clean again, and her island home was fulfilling every fantasy she'd had about it this morning. The sky was a painful crisp blue, the sand the colour of vanilla ice cream, and the sea...

Oh, how she wanted to feel that cool azure water on her skin, feel it gently stroking her limbs, easing her tension away.

She didn't allow herself to question what she did next. She just followed Finn's lead, threw her shirt and trousers on the nearest twiggy bush and, after a moment's hesitation, she peeled her vest top off, too, and hung it beside them.

The funny thing was she was used to stripping off frequently when there were quick costume changes backstage. Nobody had time to be shy then, and she honestly hadn't thought twice about it. She'd just done what had needed to be done.

But she wasn't in the wings or in a dressing room now.

And Finn wasn't one of her colleagues, used to seeing limbs and torsos as merely the machinery of his art.

She pulled herself tall and started walking towards the shore.

How strange. In her world, her lean muscles and understated curves were considered perfection, were envied even. But out here in the real world she was considered about as voluptuous as an ironing board. Dave's comment last night about Anya Pirelli had made that patently clear.

Perhaps that was why she'd been overcome by an uncharacteristic bout of shyness. Even though she knew it was impossible, that she knew he was already taken and just wouldn't look at her that way, a tiny contrary feminine part of her had wanted to impress Finn just a little bit with her toned limbs and graceful lines.

But Finn wasn't anywhere to be seen once she reached the water's edge. He'd obviously dived under. Allegra took the opportunity to submerge her body completely, even though the beach shelved gently and the sun-kissed water was only a couple of feet deep.

She closed her eyes for a moment, before walking herself deeper with her hands.

Oh, this was bliss. Perfect, perfect bliss.

When her fingers struggled to reach the bottom she opened her eyes again and began to swim, desperately, desperately trying not to notice if Finn had resurfaced or where he was.

It was no use, though. Even if he hadn't found her, if he hadn't burst from the water beside her, grinning, water running down his neck and shoulders, dragging her gaze to his powerful torso, she'd have known *exactly* where he was. The knowledge thrummed though her and made her legs shake. Unfortunately, this little mermaid was undergoing something of a species change. When Finn McLeod was around she was part woman, part jellyfish.

She let her quivering feet float to the bottom and made a

pretence of washing herself, cupping her hands and scoop-
ing up the salty water before throwing it over her shoulders
and back, and hoped fervently that her thumping heart wasn't
making little ripples in the chest-deep water that Finn might
notice.

Finn didn't notice.

He rolled onto his back and let himself float face up, his
eyes closed, and kept himself steady with the odd flap of one
of his outstretched hands.

'Isn't this perfect?' he asked quietly.

Allegra stopped washing and stared at him. She couldn't
help smiling herself as the warm sun beat down on her shoulders and the cool water lapped around her.

This man, he was so utterly different from her. He got the
urge to do something and he did it, no matter if it was crazy
or dangerous, or both. He didn't dither and second-guess himself. He made split-second decisions in high pressure situations and his gut instinct was always right. She let her breath
out slowly, hoping his ears were far enough below the surface
not to hear the ragged longing in it.

She held it again when his eyes popped open and he swivelled his head to look at her. She found an answering smile
curved her face.

'Yes, it is,' she replied softly, looking right at him. 'It *is*
perfect.'

The rest she left unsaid.

Finn clambered over a rock and then turned and thrust out
his hand for his celebrity shadow to grab. 'Not far now.' He
pulled her up onto the ledge he'd jumped up onto, then turned
to look towards the summit of the hill. 'Once we're at the top
we'll be able to get a better idea of the lie of the land.'

Allegra didn't answer. Her chest was moving rapidly and
she put her hands on her hips.

It hadn't been easy going on their trek to the island's highest point. The hill itself was nothing compared to what he was used to climbing, hardly more than a bump, but the closer they'd got to the centre of the island, the denser the jungle vegetation had become. Even for him it had been tiring.

She'd kept up, though. Had hardly even slowed him down.

It had been Dave who'd done all the moaning, despite the fact the glorious morning had meant the rest of their small crew had been able to join them and he was now guaranteed something a little more comfortable than bamboo to bed down on that night.

Allegra, however, had done everything he'd thrown at her without a murmur. She hadn't even complained about the insect bites that were popping up all over her skin, and Finn was now hastily revising his earlier conclusions about this ballerina. Her training must be a lot more rigorous than he'd imagined, because the girl had stamina. And guts.

As for blowing away in a stiff breeze? Well, he was starting to suspect it'd take something akin to a typhoon to uproot this woman if she set her mind to staying put.

A few more feet and they were standing on a broad flat rock, partially covered in yellowish grass, that marked the island's highest point. He sucked in a lungful of air. Wow. The view was stunning. He glanced over his shoulder at the crew, hoping Dave and the extra cameraman were getting some good shots.

He'd known the location of the chain of islands they'd be visiting for this episode, but other than that he knew very little about this particular spot. It had been a conscious decision on the part of both him and the production team to leave him out of the location-scouting process. That way he really had to think on his feet and use all his skills when he reached his destination. As a result, this was his first chance to see just how big the island was and what natural features it was graced with.

Allegra was standing a few feet away, turning slowly on her heels, her eyes practically popping out of her head.

'Can't beat this,' he said.

She shook her head solemnly. And then she looked right at him and gave him one of her rare smiles. Something about it reached down inside of him and he felt something like a champagne cork popping. He started to fizz with energy.

He could see it in her eyes—that she was sharing the adrenalin rush with him—that her pulse was quickening and the blood was rushing in her ears, and it reminded him of what it had felt like the first time he'd seen a view like this. How he'd been literally breathless. Somehow, knowing she was having the same rush, that first sweet taste of adventure, intensified the experience for him, too. Doubled it.

He ran to the edge of the large rock, where it rose up slightly and then dropped away suddenly for maybe forty feet into the jungle, and then he stood on his tiptoes, threw his hands out wide and yelled into the wind.

When he'd run out of breath he turned back to find the crew rolling their eyes, but Allegra...

Allegra laughed.

The sound burst from her, surprising her as much as him. She clapped her hand over her mouth to muffle it, but over the top of her fingers her eyes still danced.

Finn couldn't help but join her.

Well, blow him down if the suits back in TV land hadn't been right for once. Sharing this with someone who hadn't done it before *was* fun. It was amazing to watch her soak up everything he gave her like a sponge, to see her eyes widen in awe at each new revelation.

He ran over to her, grabbed her tiny hand and tugged her with him to the edge of the precipice.

'Have a go,' he said, grinning at her. 'There's nothing else like it.'

Her eyes sparkled, but she bit her lip and shook her head.

Finn just laughed harder, the sound rumbling low inside of him and gathering momentum until it demanded to be let out. So let it out he did.

It seemed such a shame that Allegra didn't shout her joy out, too, that he whooped again and, as he did so, he tightened his hand around hers, hoping in some small way he was taking her with him.

Allegra plunged her canteen into the cool, dark pool of water and felt the warm air bubbles rumble to the surface. When she was sure it was full she lifted it out of the water and swung it to her lips.

'No!'

Finn was through the draping ferns and beside her in a second, shoving the canteen away from her face with such force she almost dropped it. Shock must have been written all over her face, because his expression softened as he gently prised the canteen from her fingers and screwed its cap on.

'It needs to be boiled first,' he explained.

Allegra didn't do anything but stutter. Shock had given way to awareness, and Finn McLeod was standing very, very close, his dark hair flopping over his forehead and his eyes full of delicious concern.

'B-but, this…morning…'

He shook his head. 'That was rain water. Different rules.'

She nodded, even though she didn't really understand. Finn had amazed her with his ingenuity that morning. After their swim he'd set about recovering their water containers—as well as their canteens and sections of bamboo he'd cut up to make long cups—that he'd placed strategically the night before. Each one had a large rolled up leaf sticking out of the top and she'd discovered they'd acted as funnels, the torrential rain filling every one of them. But in this heat and humidity, their water supplies had gone down very fast, and there was no knowing when it would rain again.

She looked at her canteen in Finn's hands.

She'd made a rookie mistake. One that, had she really been stranded on her own, might have been fatal. It only proved how much of a fish out of water she was here—and how much she needed Finn.

Maybe Finn *had* said something about not drinking the water, but she'd been too busy watching his face light up as he'd talked about navigating their way to the head of the creek he'd spotted from the top of the island to retain that information. It turned out the spring was not far from the base of the cliff they'd been standing on earlier. But they hadn't known that until they'd made a two-hour trip, first locating the creek and then following it upstream to its source.

Finn gave her a half-apologetic, half-cheeky look, handed her canteen over and stepped back. 'Sorry if I made you jump.'

She shook her head, and then blushed hard. Finn, thankfully, had turned away to finish filling his own canteen, and Allegra was hoping the shade cast by the drooping trees would hide her heightened colour from Dave's beady-eyed lens.

It was a relief when Finn stood up and charged off into the jungle once again. She fell into step behind him, glad Dave and the rest of the crew were taking the rear and only had a clear shot of her sweat-stained back.

Their small party had doubled with the arrival of the speedboat that morning. Simon, who was both the producer and the director, had turned up, along with another cameraman—she couldn't remember his name—and a safety expert called Tim. This wasn't a big island and Allegra reckoned it was starting to feel a little crowded.

After a couple of minutes of walking, Finn stopped suddenly, eyed up a thick-trunked palm and then began hacking it to bits with his machete. Allegra quelled a shiver. There was something about a man pitting himself against nature that made a girl feel all…wobbly. When he was almost all of the way through, he pushed the trunk over and gouged a well in the stump, which instantly began to fill with clear liquid.

'Here…' he said, gesturing to it. 'If you're thirsty you can drink this.'

Allegra held back her ponytail and bent to sip from the shallow pool. The liquid tasted like water, clean and clear, with a hint of sweetness. When she'd downed as much as she could, she stood back and let Finn take a turn.

She watched him, knowing she should quench the little puddle of warmth that had begun to collect in her stomach at his thoughtful action, but she didn't have the heart.

I know he's not mine, she silently told whoever was listening. I know when this week is up we'll probably never see each other again, but let me have this. Let me have the crumbs I *can* have before I go back and face the mess I've made of my life.

Foolish girl, the ferns around her seemed to whisper. Don't unlock this gate. Don't cross this threshold.

Too late.

It was much too late for such warnings. She'd crossed into that forbidden territory when she'd started to realise Finn McLeod was so much more than a two-dimensional fantasy. She'd instantly lost herself in that new place when she'd seen that the flesh and blood man was so much more than pixels of light on a TV screen.

The territory of teenage crush was rapidly being left behind, and Allegra had no idea where she was heading now—only that it was new and frightening and exhilarating all at the same time, and that she had no choice but to follow him, because finally she felt alive.

'Better now?'

Finn had finished, and his voice beside her ear roused her

from her fanciful ramblings. She shut the door on them, not wanting to probe too deeply into what was happening to her, anyway. All she wanted to do was enjoy one week with Finn McLeod. Surely that wasn't too much to ask?

Or was that just wishful thinking, that same disease that had plagued the character she'd brought to life on stage less than a week ago? Mermaid thinking. And that girl hadn't really known when to give up and let go of the dream, had she? She'd let her hopeless desire for the wrong guy rob her of her very life.

'Much better,' she said, ignoring that thought. 'How long until we reach our camp?'

Finn scrunched up his face and peered into the never-ending greenness in front of them. While he was working it out, her empty stomach decided to voice its displeasure with a loud and rather unladylike growl.

'About an hour,' he said, turning back to her. And then he smiled. 'Why don't we see if we can find some food along the way?'

CHAPTER SIX

'How about a snack?' Finn asked and waited for Allegra's answer.

Dave, who had been on enough adventures with Finn to know exactly what sort of snack might be on the menu, positioned himself and his camera accordingly.

'I'm ravenous,' she said quickly.

Good. With what he had in mind, she'd need to be.

He kicked the rotted fallen tree he'd found with his boot and watched it crumble. Just as he'd hoped, when he cleared the bark away he found some grubs squirming there, bright and pearly-white against the dark wood. He picked a couple up and popped them in his mouth as if they were lemon drops.

'Great source of protein,' he said, before biting down into the firm flesh, feeling everything squelch out. He then got it down as quickly as possible. He grinned at his disciple, hoping he'd convince her to give them a go. No point in telling her they tasted like feet.

From the look on Allegra's face, Finn knew that if she'd had any breakfast this morning, this would have been the point when she would have lost it.

He picked another wriggling grub up and offered it to her. She took a large step back.

Come on, Allegra. You've surprised me at every turn so far today. Don't buck the trend and disappoint me.

'You said you were ravenous.'

Allegra didn't respond. She was too busy staring at the small creature tickling his palm.

'It's no big deal,' he added, conveniently pushing aside his first memory of doing the same, when he'd decorated a fellow soldier's boots.

'I know you can do this,' he said, lowering his voice to coax her further. 'You've got it in you. All you need to do is *choose* to believe you can.'

Her eyes flicked up and held his gaze with an intensity that startled him. She inched a little closer. Not much, but a little.

'Do *you* believe I can?' She said it quietly and if he hadn't known any better, he'd have thought he'd detected a tremble in her voice.

He glanced down at the grub, still blissfully unaware of its potential fate, and then back at her.

'Yes,' he said simply, knowing he was telling the truth.

Allegra's mouth twitched as if he'd said something funny. Something funny and slightly wonderful. 'You really believe I've got it in me to pick up this…*thing*…pop it in my mouth and chew?'

He nodded. 'Yes. One hundred per cent.'

Something odd happened then. Her eyes sparkled, just as they'd done when she'd been standing on top of the island, drinking in all the beauty. They were full of wonder and promise and something else he couldn't quite put his finger on. Didn't matter, though. She looked amazing.

Without blinking, trapping him with her eyes, she pinched the grub between thumb and forefinger and threw it into her mouth. No hesitation. Then she clamped her lips together and moved her jaw.

He saw on her face the moment the larvae exploded and she got the full experience, but she didn't open her mouth and spit anything out until her throat had moved and the 'snack' was gone. Then she braced her hands on her knees, bent over and coughed and spluttered.

Finn felt a pang of guilt as he clapped her on the back. 'Probably should have warned you about the taste, huh?' he said.

'You don't say,' Allegra replied hoarsely before pulling herself upright again.

Finn laughed.

Brave, and funny, too.

Allegra Martin was shaping up to be the perfect castaway companion.

Allegra eyed the night vision camera bolted to the tree opposite the shelter entrance suspiciously. 'How much can that thing actually see?' she asked Finn as he dumped yet another bundle of palm leaves into her waiting arms.

He shrugged. 'Everything. Why?'

She turned and spread the dry leaves on the top of the bamboo poles. This was at least the third layer. Finn had better be telling the truth about it being more comfortable this way. If she found out it was going to be as 'okay' as eating the bug had been, she'd kill him with his own machete.

A shudder ran up her spine and she couldn't help wiping her tongue against her lips a few times. She could still taste the vile little creature, and she hated to think what it must have excreted inside her mouth to make it taste so bad. She shuddered again.

'No reason,' she replied as she finished spreading the leaves across the shelter floor.

'That means you've got to behave yourself!' he added. It was just a throwaway comment—he didn't even look at her. Nothing in it. Just one of Finn's jokes.

Instantly she spun back around and played with the bedding, flushing hot and cold. 'You should be so lucky,' she muttered, doing a passable imitation of not at all bothered.

She didn't want to banter like this with Finn, even if it showed he was starting to feel comfortable around her. Teasing was too close to flirting, and flirting was too close to pretending she could have all the things that could never be hers.

Chore finished, she straightened and then headed down to the beach, stopping where the dry sand ended. The sun was starting to set, and since their beach faced west she had a ringside view. It made something inside her ache. But in a good way. As if something unused and stiff was waking up.

She sighed. An inadequate response, but it was all she had.

The crew's speedboat had left more than twenty minutes ago, but she couldn't quite bring herself to stay close to Finn unless she had to. She let out a hollow little laugh. How totally gauche and pathetic she was. Alone on a desert island with the man of her dreams. She knew plenty of girls who'd jump at the chance to jump onto Finn McLeod, fiancée or no fiancée, but unfortunately she couldn't.

No. Actually, she *wouldn't*. Her choice.

Because she didn't want Finn to be the sort of man who'd cave so easily when temptation arrived on his doorstep. Because she thought she'd shrivel up and die if he replied, *Yeah, honey. Let's have a steamy tropical fling.* He wouldn't be the man she believed him to be then. At least this way she still had the *idea* of Finn to cherish.

She shook her head and concentrated on the descending orange disc on the horizon. That at least was all she had hoped it would be. However, the moment it disappeared completely she was forced to retreat up the beach. Night fell quickly here and she needed to get back to the warmth and light of the huge fire they'd built. And Finn, of course.

He'd stoked it up nicely and was cooking some fish he'd caught by sharpening a length of slim bamboo and splitting the end into a star-shaped spear. Allegra was surprised just how filling one fish, some boiled roots Finn had dug up on

the trek back to camp and half a coconut could be. Once her
stomach was full, her eyelids began to droop.

She stifled a yawn with the back of her hand. When she
opened her eyes again, Finn was looking at her.

'It's been quite a day,' he said seriously.

No kidding.

'I reckon it's time to hit the ferns,' he added.

Allegra just nodded and dragged herself into the shelter,
leaving her head at the open end near the fire. What a difference to the previous night! She was warm and dry and Finn,
thankfully for him, had been right about the jungle mattress.
Not that she'd have had much energy to do anything about it
if he hadn't.

She rolled onto her back and felt the bamboo poles beside
her bounce as Finn joined her. She turned her head to say
goodnight and found him staring up at the stars beyond the
roof of the shelter and grinning like a loon. The firelight cast
soft shadows on his face and he looked simply adorable.

'You really love what you do, don't you?' she said sleep-
ily.

'Uh-huh.' He nodded, still staring at the star-sprinkled
sky. 'Don't you?'

That question sobered her up from her sleepy stupor a lit-
tle bit. Back home, her standard response would have been,
Of course. But here… Everything was too open, too honest.
She found she couldn't lie.

'Sometimes,' she said slowly. 'Sometimes I hate it, too.'
She paused for a few breaths. 'Mostly I hate it.'

Finn frowned and rolled over to prop himself on one elbow.
'Why do you do something you hate?'

Allegra looked away and stared at the orange shadows
dancing on the roof of the shelter for a long time.

'Sometimes you have to do what's expected of you. I mean,
you must have to do certain things to continue to be the pre-

senter of *Fearless Finn,* don't you? And if you didn't, you'd be letting people down.'

She moved her head just enough to catch his reaction out of the corner of her eye.

'True,' he said, nodding again. 'So…who *expected* you to be a prima ballerina?'

Oh, that question was easy. So easy she let out a little dry laugh. 'Everyone!'

Finn laughed, too. And when he realised she wasn't joking, he stopped.

'Ever since I put on my first pair of ballet shoes, people watched me closely,' she said. 'They watched, they waited, trying to see if I had the same gift as my mother. It pleased everyone—especially her—that I did. She died when I was eight and afterwards I felt it connected me to her. It felt as if I was talking to her when I was dancing.' She wrinkled her nose and allowed herself to look at him more fully. 'That sounds silly, doesn't it?'

'No.' Finn looked back at her, the most serious she'd ever seen him. 'It sounds as if you were a little girl who missed her mother.'

Strangely, that thought made Allegra smile. Finn had such a clear, practical way of saying things. No oblique hints, no subtext. He knew what he wanted to say and he said it. But he didn't ramble or stutter. It was rather impressive.

She frowned as she tried to do the same—tried to put clear words to the half-acknowledged feelings that had been weighing her down for so long.

'I grew up believing ballet was what I loved more than anything, but I think I confused it with the memory of my mother. Now I'm not sure if I ever loved it at all. It asks too much. More than I have to give.'

She stopped talking, waited for the bottom to fall out of the universe at her admission, but in the breathless seconds that followed nothing happened. The planet remained on its axis. There were no mighty heaven-rending explosions. All she could hear was the shuffle of the surf against the shore and the crackle of the fire. And if Finn was shocked at her outburst, he was hiding it very well.

Allegra felt a huge weight lift off her.

There. She'd finally said it. And it had been so easy.

'I always thought I had chosen ballet but, looking back, I can see my path was chosen for me. It was my mother's dream, not mine. But I wore it with pride, just like the sapphire brooch she left me.' She closed her eyes before she said the rest. 'I feel so ungrateful, because I know there are hundreds of dancers who'd kill for my life. It's horrible to be blessed with a gift you don't really want but have the responsibility of living up to.'

Finn's voice was soft and warm in the darkness. 'Give it up. Find something you're passionate about. Life's too short, Allegra.'

She opened her lids and stared at him long and hard. He was serious, wasn't he? She swallowed. Even a week ago, if someone had said that to her she'd have laughed at the impossibility of it. Right now, she wasn't even smiling.

Could she? Could she walk away and be free?

She didn't know. Wasn't sure she had the strength. It was easy for someone like Finn to say such a thing.

She rolled onto her left side and faced him, mirrored his position with her head propped on her hand. 'I'm not like you,' she said softly. 'I wish I was, though.'

Finn grinned at her. 'You wish you were twice your current weight, widely acknowledged to be slightly bonkers and in need of a good shave?'

Allegra grinned back. 'No,' she said, scolding him good-naturedly. 'I mean it would be nice to be spur-of-the-moment, spontaneous…creative.'

Finn looked shocked. 'You're a ballet dancer! Of course you're creative!'

She shook her head. 'I don't make up the moves. I just dance them. I don't have the luxury of *choosing* my steps. I just follow instructions.'

Finn pressed his lips into a grudging smile. 'Nah, don't buy it. I've seen you dance.' His gaze shifted to the starry sky again as he pulled the memory from its filing place, and then he looked back at her. 'I saw you dance Juliet—Nat dragged me along.' He gave her a look that reminded her of a naughty schoolboy. 'That sounded awful. Sorry.'

She tried not to smile back, and failed. 'Forgiven.'

'But you're wrong when you say you're not spontaneous and creative. You took that choreography and filled it with life. You made it something unique.'

Allegra's whole body began to tingle, warmed by Finn's praise, then as suddenly as the pins and needles had started, they vanished.

'That was a long time ago.' She looked at the mattress beneath her fingers, played with a thin leaf. 'Don't you read the papers? I've burned out since then. Lost my spark.'

Finn didn't say anything and her stomach went cold, fearing his silence, but when she found the courage to meet his gaze she discovered he'd been waiting for her to do just that. He dismissed her comment with a word that shouldn't be repeated in polite company.

'I don't believe that. Not from what I've seen of you in the last two days. But it really doesn't matter what the papers think. It's what you think that counts.'

Allegra raised her eyebrows. What a novel concept.

Finn continued. 'I think you need to stop waiting to see if ballet has finished with you and decide if you have finished with *it*. It's your choice, Allegra. Yours alone.'

Neither of them said anything for a long time after that. Finn left her to digest what he'd said in peace, and digest it she did. Who knew if it would agree with her?

I don't know about ballet, she silently told him, *but you're my choice. That one was easy. Took no effort at all.*

When she sneaked a look at him again his eyelids were closed, and seeing him give in to drowsiness pulled her own lids down, too. She let them slide closed as she rolled over, but before sleep took over she whispered, 'Thank you, Finn.'

'No problem' was the mumbled reply.

And then Allegra wasn't aware of anything any more.

'Doesn't this make you wish we had a packet of marshmallows?' Finn was enjoying the contrast of the warmth from the fire on his face and front and cool night snaking up his back under his shirt. With a million childhood campfires swirling in his head he turned to Allegra, who was sitting on a log they'd pulled close to the fire for a bench, looking at him with blank eyes. He poked the fire with the stick he'd been holding before dropping it into the flames.

'You never went camping as a kid?' he asked, almost wondering if such a horror could be true.

She shook her head.

Wow. A deprived childhood indeed, despite her obviously cultured and privileged background.

'Not even once?'

She bit her lip and shrugged. Finn tried hard to find the silver lining. He liked silver linings; they protected a man from the depressing facts of life. His gaze roamed to the shelter, the fire, the moonlit beach and then he turned back to her. 'At least this week should go some way to making up for that.'

She smiled at that. 'Apart from the marshmallows,' she added quietly.

Right then and there, Finn decided to send a whole crate of marshmallows to Allegra when he got back to London. Then she could use her fire-making skills to roast them whenever she liked—if she ever managed to get the knack of it, of course.

'Who did you go camping with?' she asked. 'Your parents?'

Finn nodded. 'Sometimes. But I used to spend a huge chunk of my summer holidays with my grandfather at his home on Skye. We'd go camping and fishing and hill-walking...'

Allegra sat up a little. 'And marshmallows were always essential kit?'

'Always,' Finn replied, grinning. 'Grandad would eat the pink ones and I'd eat the white.'

She laughed. 'Why no pink ones for you? Too girly?'

Finn drew breath, intending to give a lengthy, and completely fictional, account of why pink sweets would never threaten his masculinity; but then he saw her gaze sharpen with intelligence and he just gave up and nodded. That made her laugh even harder.

'I can relate to that,' she said, sighing. 'My whole childhood was a rhapsody in pink. Pink tights, pink shoes, pink leotards... It got to the point where I would positively avoid it unless I was in class or on stage.'

He watched her as she trailed off and gazed into the fire. Pink was okay. Beautiful in a sunset or a rainforest flower. But life was made to be full of colour. Surely that amount of uniformity couldn't be good for a soul?

They really came from two different worlds, didn't they? He was always on the move, always filling himself up with new experiences from one day to the next, and yet she had got where she was by *staying*. By doing the same thing over and over until she reached perfection. How did she do it without going stark raving mad?

She leaned forward and rested her chin on her fist. 'He must be really proud of you.'

Finn sat down on the opposite end of the log. 'Who?'

She smiled gently. 'Your grandfather.'

He found he couldn't look at the softness in those blue

eyes any more and turned his attention back to the crackling logs. Why had he dropped that stick? He really needed to prod those logs with it and now he had nothing to hand.

'He died when I was fifteen.'

She didn't say anything for a moment, but Finn could feel her sympathy radiating towards him along the log. He knew she'd suffered worse, knew she'd understand, but he still didn't want to share it with her. Letting her in meant he'd have to visit that place himself, and he'd boarded it up and marked it 'no entry' a long time ago.

'I'm sorry,' she said.

There it was. That beguiling compassion made into words. It made him feel as if a thousand spiders had just started climbing his legs.

He stood up. 'Don't worry about it,' he said, not looking at her.

She shouldn't. He never did.

Why buck the trend? He hadn't thought to worry at all that Christmas they'd spent the whole week at Grandad's. Hadn't paid a lick of attention when his grandfather had hugged him goodbye and said, 'See you in the summer'. On the next visit to Skye, only a few short months later, hiking boots and waterproofs had been traded for a dark suit and smart shoes. Wild heather and open skies had been replaced by wreaths and the claustrophobic stillness of a tiny chapel.

He *should* have worried, though.

He should have realised how much his only living grandparent had been an anchoring point for him throughout his childhood. Should have realised how set adrift he'd feel once the old man was gone.

People thought the wilderness was empty. They were blind. It was full of life—plants, trees, creatures big enough to swallow you whole or so small they were almost invisible to the naked eye. Absent of human interference, yes, but not empty.

No, emptiness was standing at a graveside and not even

being able to look at the coffin because all you could see was the hole. All you could *feel* was the hole. Blackness so complete that it wiped out all life before it. *That* was emptiness.

Not a place he ever planned on visiting again, thank goodness.

Allegra stood up. For a moment he thought she was going to move closer and hug him. He was very glad when she didn't.

'Some people leave big spaces when they go,' she whispered, almost to herself rather than to him. 'Shoes you can never—'

She paused for a moment.

'Sorry. I meant *holes* you can never fill, no matter how hard you try.'

Finn walked over to a bush and broke a decent-looking branch off it, then he stripped it of all its smaller twigs and plunged it into the licking orange flames. He didn't say anything because he didn't want to agree with her. That would be lying.

He'd filled in all his holes a long time ago. You could hardly tell they'd been there in the first place. Anchors made holes. Roots made holes. But he'd learned since then that if he moved fast enough he could avoid those kinds of cavities entirely. As a result, his life was always full, never empty.

But then he made the mistake of glancing up at her. Just the look in her eyes ripped something inside of him. And he couldn't have that. Those tiny breaches in the shell were how it started.

He glanced towards the shelter. 'I don't know about you, but I'm ready for sleep,' he said and, before Allegra could answer he dropped his stick, clambered over the log and headed for the palm leaf mattress.

Something was gently nudging Allegra's shoulder. She rolled over to escape it and crashed into something solid. Something warm. Something that was whispering her name…

She slowly heaved her eyelids open and tried to focus on

the shape directly in front of her face. She thought it might be Finn. Her racing pulse told her it was but, instead of having two eyes, this Finn had one large fuzzy one in the middle of his face.

'Good morning,' the eye said.

Allegra tried to answer, but the only thing that escaped her lips was a string of consonants, none of them logically connected to the previous one.

'I take it you slept well.'

More consonants. Ones that were supposed to string together to mean: 'Maybe not *well,* but *better.*'

Some part of Allegra's brain that had still been dozing suddenly decided to sit up and take notice. She was nose to nose with Finn McLeod in the semi-dark! How had that happened?

'It's time to catch breakfast,' he said.

'Smoked salmon bagel and a cappuccino, please,' she said in a scratchy voice, not quite ready to pull away from him.

'Funny lady,' he said, and the eye grew smaller and clearer and separated into two.

Come back, Allegra wanted to whisper. *Come back and place your lips close to mine again. Let me believe they were just about to touch.*

She didn't, of course, despite the fact her sleep fog was making her want to do things she wouldn't normally do. Or wouldn't normally *admit* to wanting to do.

'You were right about the fish part, though,' Finn said. 'This is a good time of day to catch them hiding in the shallows.'

Allegra's brain told her to say, *Stuff the fish!* and hold out for the bagel. Her stomach, however, mounted a rebellion and made her push herself up to sit cross-legged on the mattress of ferns and palm leaves.

'Come on,' Finn said, and reached across to ruffle her sleep-styled hair further. And then he launched himself out of the shelter and started coaxing the still-glowing embers from the previous night back to life.

She closed her eyes and resisted the urge to howl in frustration.

He sees me as a kid sister! she wailed inside her head. *Nothing more.*

And why should he? You're far too young for him. And he has a fiancée.

Allegra squeezed her eyes closed harder and clenched her teeth. *I know, I know. Shut up!*

Then she opened her eyes and saw Finn striding down the beach, spear in hand. It felt as if her foolish heart jumped straight out of her chest and scurried on down the beach after him, like a waggy little dog.

Silently, she called it back, even though she knew it was no use.

She sighed and buried her face in her hands. She'd thought she'd known what longing was before she'd reached this island, had she?

Wrong!

So totally, totally wrong.

And now she recognised that emotion for what it was, knew its depths, she had the feeling it had the power to turn this island paradise into a living hell.

Allegra had never known damnation could be so sweet. Despite the rigorous physical work it took just to eat and drink and live on this island, she pushed herself to stay awake as long as possible in the evenings, because that was when she and Finn would talk about anything and everything. And she forced herself to consciousness early in the mornings, just so she could snatch a few extra minutes with him before the crew arrived. And he seemed to enjoy her company as much as she enjoyed his.

Her body complained, of course. She ignored it. She was

used to pushing it to its limits. At least ballet had given her that.

Every second with Finn counted, because now they were practically halfway through their week together. From now on, time would haemorrhage, slowly leaking away, until the helicopter appeared on the horizon to separate her from Finn. Possibly for ever.

Yes, it *should* be for ever. She knew that.

He had a fiancée to go home to, and seeing him back in the real world would just be too difficult, so she was going to go cold turkey once the filming was over. All she could have was this perfect little bubble of time with him, and have it she would.

It was day four and they had just climbed out of the shelter to start the day. First job was to get the fire started, using the wood they had collected and heaped up in readiness the evening before. Finn was trying to teach Allegra how to do it on her own. A useful skill, he'd said.

Useful for him, maybe, Allegra had thought.

She could imagine the outrage she'd cause amongst her Notting Hill neighbours if she decided to start a campfire in the leafy garden square outside her father's house.

That didn't stop her, though. She *wanted* to learn this. Not just to impress Finn, but to prove something to herself.

The materials were ready—tinder, kindling, larger logs for fuel—and she'd placed it all just-so, ready for an ember to ignite. Finn had declared it a perfect set-up. But could she get the knife and flint to generate a spark to set it all off? No, she could not. And it was driving her crazy.

She placed the flint on the tinder once again and struck the knife against it with force. Nothing. She wanted to scream.

Finn, who was crouching down beside her, laid a hand on her arm. 'You're really close, but why don't you let me finish off?'

'No!'

Whoops. That had come out a little more stroppily than she'd intended it to. She'd better get herself under control; the rest of the crew would be here shortly, and this was not how she wanted the world to see her—as a spoilt little princess having a paddy. Running away without telling anyone would have created that impression of her, anyway, and she wasn't about to do anything that might give the press fuel for *their* fire.

'I want to do it myself,' she said, a little more graciously.

'And I want to eat today,' Finn muttered good-naturedly, but he removed his hand from her arm and sat back down on the thick log they'd dragged beside the fire pit for a bench.

So she tried again. And again. And another twelve times after that.

Finn's tone was far too reasonable when he said, 'You're trying too hard.'

She put the knife down and swivelled on her haunches to face him.

'Yesterday you said I had to stop—and I quote—"messing around with it". Make up your mind!'

When she'd finished snapping at him she clamped her mouth shut. What was wrong with her today? She couldn't seem to get a handle on her frustration as she usually did.

Luckily, Finn being Finn, he saw the funny side. And he didn't seem to be insulted in the least by her sulky outburst.

After a few more tries, she joined him on the log and handed the tools over. Then she propped her elbows on her knees and sank her face into her hands and watched him get to work. He made it look so easy. As if it was like breathing for him.

'What I mean is—' Finn broke off as he concentrated on striking knife against flint. Sparks flew. Lots of them. Not something Finn McLeod was short of, obviously. Within a few seconds he was juggling a loose ball of dry grass and flames were licking through it, threatening to scorch his fingers. He

dropped it carefully in the fire pit and began assembling the
wood around it, talking as he did so.

'I know it seems strange to put it like this, but I've always thought of fire as a living thing. Making fire is more
than just following instructions; you need a bit of instinct,
too—knowing just when and where to strike the flint, and
how hard. Knowing when to trust the ember you've got and
blow, or knowing it's not strong enough and the only thing
that blowing would do is put it out.'

Great. Instinct again. Inner spark. The stuff Allegra was
all out of. Maybe she'd never get this right.

She tried not to care about that as they fished and ate
breakfast. She tried not to care when the film crew arrived
and Dave pointed his all-seeing lens at her. Most of all she
tried not to care when they took their daily hike through the
thick vegetation to fetch water from the pool.

But she did care. A lot.

Because Finn had said *spark* was important, the thing
you needed in spades if you were ever going to survive. And
Allegra had the feeling she hadn't been surviving. Not even
when she'd been back in London.

On their journey they walked past the tree stump that Finn
had plucked the grubs from the other day. He looked over his
shoulder and gave her a cheeky grin, raised his eyebrows in a
question. She scowled at him and shook her head. The crew
behind her chuckled.

But as she continued to follow Finn, Allegra began to consider something she'd forgotten—Finn McLeod thought she
had *spark*. He'd said so.

He could be wrong, of course. Mistaken. But she'd eaten
the darn bug anyway. Surely that had to count for something?

She desperately wanted it to.

Maybe he was right. Maybe it was all locked away inside
and she didn't know how to get to it any more. Perhaps that
was why she was so obsessed with creating fire. If she could

do that, maybe she could believe she could take all the other things Finn had taught her home and put her mess of a life into order.

Or was that just a hopeless fantasy? As pathetic as yearning for a future with Finn. The dread plagued her all the way to the pool, cramping her shoulder muscles and tensing her jaw. Even the multitude of insect bites dotting her skin seemed to throb and itch more insistently.

After they'd filled their various containers, Finn suggested a detour back to the top of the island. Now they knew the way, it would only be another twenty minutes hiking. Allegra nodded and trudged after him. Maybe getting out of the oppressive heat and humidity of the jungle and standing in the fresh air and sunshine would improve her mood.

It didn't.

As beautiful as it all was, it didn't. She stood on the edge of the small cliff, staring out at the lush landscape, the shimmering sea, and it didn't help one bit.

'Hey,' Finn said from right behind her, practically whispering in her left ear.

See? This proved just how off-kilter she was. She hadn't even sensed his approach.

'You're as rigid as one of these rocks,' he said. And then he placed his hands on her shoulders and began to knead. Oh, my, he began to knead. Firmly. Smoothly. Expertly.

Allegra closed her eyes, glad none of the crew had a shot of her face, and stifled a whimper.

Was it better to pull away and deprive herself of this, never to have a hint of what it could be like, or would it be better to savour it while it lasted, even if it was sweet torture? She didn't know. And the indecision paralysed her body while making her head spin. And Finn's hands…? They were slowly turning her muscles to heated, sticky marshmallow.

Why had fate dangled him in front of her before pulling

him away again? She wanted to scream at the unfairness of it all.

Her eyelids had drifted open a little and she spotted the small outcrop Finn had stood on the other day. She didn't decide to move; she just did. She ran to the little pointy bit of rock, planted her feet where his had been and let all the frustration and self-pity that had been building in her like a pressure cooker out in one long howl.

Time did something strange. She lost all awareness of how long it took the sound to leave her body, the air to vacate her lungs, and yet she became hyper-aware of the accompanying physical sensations—the heat at the back of her throat, the contraction of her intercostal and abdominal muscles, the way the air seemed to come from right down behind her belly button instead of her chest.

After all that noise, the following silence was thick and complete. She suddenly remembered where she was and—oh, no—who she was with. Was there any chance they'd been changing tapes while she'd had her moment of insanity?

She glanced round to find the entire crew staring at her, some of them with their mouths open. So she hitched her chin, tucked a stray bit of hair behind her ear and fixed her eyes on the one solid thing in her universe at the moment: Finn McLeod. He was also staring, but his eyes were laughing and that did something strange to her.

'You're right,' she said, surprising herself by sounding as cool and poised and elegant as a ballerina was supposed to. 'I do feel better now.'

And then she began to vocalise what she saw in Finn's eyes. She began to laugh. No gentle, polite tittering, either. Big, helpless, gulping peals that made her feel dizzy.

Somehow Finn was standing beside her, joining her, laughing just as hard as she was. Before they'd fully recovered, he sputtered out a question: 'You want to do that again?'

She nodded.

That was all he needed. He grabbed her hand and they both rose onto their tiptoes, threw their heads back and yelled.

Finn felt as if he could leap off the cliff and fly. Surely, with this soaring feeling inside it would finally be possible? Not even gravity could stop them. The wind would carry them and the warm thermals would buoy them up. He and Allegra could just close their eyes and dive off the cliff into the ultimate freedom. Because he knew he wanted her with him.

Look at her! Where had the clenched little ballerina he'd shared a helicopter ride with gone? Her cheeks were pink and her eyes were shiny. In a sudden burst of clarity he understood why some people paid hundreds of pounds just for the pleasure of watching her all evening.

He realised that even though he'd thought she was beautiful when she danced, he hadn't known anything. This was way better, because this time he wasn't just a spectator, but a participant. They'd joined together and she'd taken him with her on her leap into uncharted territory.

And, as the pounding of his heart subsided, as he watched her standing there, silent now, eyes closed, face to the sun, he realised something else—he very badly wanted to kiss her.

CHAPTER SEVEN

Finn was staring at her, shock written on every single feature, but it was quickly erased and replaced by a frown. Allegra's stomach felt as if it had plummeted to the bottom of the small cliff. Had she gone too far?

She must have done. Look at his face.

No one who knew the reserved, quiet, unapproachable Allegra Martin back in London would have believed she would have even raised her voice, let alone yelled until her throat was sore and then laughed like a crazy woman.

Maybe she was having a breakdown.

Yes, that must be it. How else could she explain running away to spend a week on a desert island in the middle of a production? And all the not-Allegra type things she'd done since?

But how could this be madness? How could this be wrong? She'd never felt so free. And if sanity was what she'd had before, she wasn't sure she wanted it back.

She looked at Finn. Instead of the confident, can-do-anything grin he normally wore, his mouth was slightly open and he was looking a little pale. Did he think that what she'd just done had wandered from *fun* into something…well, more *diagnosable?* Was that why he'd gone so quiet?

'Finn, are you okay?'

No mischievous grin, no witty comeback. He merely nodded and turned to face the four men standing on the other end of the rocky peak. 'Time we got back down to camp and started thinking about food for this evening.'

And then he scrambled down the rocky slope without waiting for her or the crew. It was almost a full two minutes before they caught up with him.

He was weird all the way back to camp, too. Didn't point out one edible or medicinal plant en route, or catch large wriggling insects and hold them up to the camera. Just kept walking until his feet met sand, and then he threw his boots off and marched into the sea, fully clothed.

Allegra put her hands on her hips and watched him swim furiously until he reached the little rock island with the tree on top, where he hauled himself out of the water and sat down under the sparsely leaved branches and stared out to sea.

Nobody followed him. Not even Dave. To be honest, from the way the crew were looking at each other and shuffling from foot to foot, she'd guess they were just as puzzled as she was.

Maybe she wasn't the only one going bananas.

He stayed on the island for half an hour. Until he felt a little bit closer to normal. If he hadn't had to worry about a filming schedule and a celebrity guest star, he might have stayed out there all night.

Where on earth had *that* come from?

One minute he'd been excited about his protégé's progress, about her courage to do something way beyond her comfort zone, and the next…?

Well, it hadn't been an eager student standing beside him, but a captivating woman, one who had so much more potential than she realised, and his testosterone had gone into overdrive. All she'd done was smile at him, and he'd been able to see the thrill of new experiences fresh on her lips, and he'd wanted to *share* it, to *taste* it.

And then he hadn't felt as if he was flying any more, but falling. Into a big dark hole with no way out. That was when he'd started running.

Whatever was going on here was definitely not a good idea.

He'd only just been dumped by his long-term fiancée. Chances were that this was probably just a rebound thing— a reflex. A long-buried caveman instinct to prove himself by finding another woman. Not very evolved, to be sure. But, hey, he was a guy. Not much he could do about that.

He stood up, brushed down the back of his trousers and looked back towards the beach.

It wouldn't be a good idea to pursue this *thing* with Allegra.

He had a job to do. And they were in each other's company every hour of every day for the rest of the week. Hothouse conditions. The result was spectacular, yes, but things were unnaturally accelerated in that kind of environment. There'd be no breathing room, no escape, if things got out of control. Better to leave well enough alone. For both their sakes.

That sorted in his head, he decided he was ready to go back to the beach and face the crew.

What about Allegra? a little voice inside his head said.

What about her? She's a female of the species, yes. I've noticed that now. But I'm not so devoid of self-control that I can't spend time with her without behaving myself. All I can ever *share* with her is my skills, my training. And I can share the next three days on this island with her and that will be that.

Good luck with that, the voice said.

Finn ignored it.

He jumped into the turquoise water and swam back to shore at a leisurely pace.

Allegra was collecting firewood. The rest of the crew seemed to be occupied, but the atmosphere was a little too incurious, a little too nonchalant. However, at this present moment, nonchalance suited him just fine, so he went with it.

Dave was the only one to show concern. Trust Dave. Couldn't he have grumbled about the unexpected jog through the jungle back to the beach?

'You okay?' he said.

'Fine,' said Finn, grinning. His face felt artificial. 'You know me. I'm a bit of a loner at times, and I just needed a bit of solitude to recharge my batteries. All charged up now, though…' And then he surprised himself by dancing around like a boxer to prove it, even jabbed Dave playfully on the shoulder. What *was* he doing?

'Yippee,' Dave said, returning to normal. He gave Finn a look that said, *Try that again, mate, and you'll be fish food.*

'Okay,' Finn said, clapping his hands together, aware his voice was very loud in his own ears. 'Next thing we're going to do is take a more in-depth look at cordage, what kind of ropes can be made from the plants that occur naturally in a habitat like this.'

The crew mumbled out a sarcastic cheer.

Finn turned to the woman he'd avoided looking at so far, who was crouching on the ground, piling kindling for that evening's fire. 'Allegra?'

His heart began to thump. Don't think about it, he told himself.

His smile stayed fixed on his lips and he managed to do just that. For a few seconds. Allegra looked up at him with those big, transparent, unblinking blue eyes. His gaze slid to her lips. She wasn't smiling with them now. Wasn't doing anything special at all with them, really. It should have been safe.

But all Finn could think about was how much he really wanted to taste and share.

Finn kept everyone busy all afternoon. They must have collected enough firewood to last them at least two days, and he wasted another hour trying—and mostly failing—to build a raft that fell apart and dunked him in the sea as soon as it encountered a big wave. The crew had found the whole episode highly entertaining.

He tried hard not to think if his celebrity sidekick found it funny. He was trying very hard not to think about her at all. But now and then he forgot himself and glanced in her direction. Each time he saw exactly the same thing: Allegra staring back at him with a hint of bewilderment in her big blue eyes.

In the end he decided to put those eyes where he couldn't see them—behind him—and suggested a trek to the other end of the island, where it sharpened into a point. When they'd stood on top of the hill, he thought he'd seen evidence of human occupation at some point, and he wanted to see if he was right.

He'd been spot-on.

There was a ruin there—a stone fort, it looked like. He guessed it had probably been built by the Spanish a few hundred years ago to fend off the pirates who'd wanted to steal their New World gold. Only one wall remained intact, about six feet high, in an L-shape. The rest of the structure had succumbed to the creepers and grass that had pushed between the stones.

He warbled to camera about the history of the area for at least half an hour, even though he knew Simon probably wouldn't use it. But when the sun started to dip in the sky he reluctantly made the call to return to camp. Once there, he stuck close to the camera crew until they escaped in their tiny white speedboat.

I'm not being cowardly, he told himself. I'm just being sensible. Better to put up a few barriers to protect himself—protect both of them—from one of his sudden and often irresistible urges. Having a dive-in-first, ask-questions-later kind of personality could be an asset in some survival situations, but when it came to relationships he'd learned the hard way that slowly and carefully was the only way to go.

The sun was now setting, and there was an awfully long time to kill before the crew returned in the morning. He poked the fire with a large stick and racked his brain for a plan. Thankfully, it didn't take long.

'How do you fancy going for a walk?' he said, not looking at his sole companion, but concentrating on a glowing bit of timber he was bothering with his makeshift poker. Sparks flew and whirled up into the air.

'A *walk?*'

'Mmm-hmm.'

'But it's dark,' she said. He could hear the frown in her voice. Knew her eyebrows had dipped in the middle as they always did when she was uncertain about something.

'I have a plan,' he said, and then went about showing her just how easy it was to make a torch out of a decent-sized stick and some combustible material lashed to the top. Thank goodness, after this afternoon's mini-lecture on cordage, they had plenty of the stuff lying around.

He made a torch for each of them, dipped them in the fire long enough for them to billow bright flames, and then they set off across the beach towards the headland. Never had Finn been so glad his guest star was a woman of few words.

But as they neared the rock-punctuated sand at the end of the beach, Allegra opened her mouth and spoke.

'I have a confession to make,' she said carefully. 'I should have told you earlier, really, but at first home seemed so far away—both in time and space—but now I've suddenly realised I'm only days away from being back there again.'

'Uh-huh.' That was right. Keep it light and non-committal. 'Well…'

Allegra slowed even further. Finn didn't look at her face, but watched her feet make tiny, delicate dents in the sand.

'I thought I'd better warn you that there might be a bit of

fallout from me being a guest on *Fearless Finn.* Maybe not for you,' she added quickly. 'But definitely for me.'

Finn was so intrigued he forgot he was trying not to look her directly in the eye. He stopped walking and turned to face her. 'How so?'

Allegra looked down at her feet and traced a tiny precise arc in the sand with her big toe. 'I did something stupid.'

Finn knew all about stupid. It was his speciality, his father used to say. 'What sort of stupid? Locked your keys in the car stupid, or fallen off a cliff stupid?'

She sighed and her gaze flicked up to meet his. 'Definitely the latter.'

He took a few steps up the beach until he was beyond the tide line, plunged the non-flaming end of his torch into the soft sand and sat down. He motioned for her to do the same. They sat about three feet apart, both facing the ocean, with their knees up, staring out into the darkness, trying to figure out where sea met night sky.

'When I left I didn't tell anyone where I was going, and—' she swallowed '—I was supposed to be performing this evening.'

He swung round to look at her. She didn't mirror him but kept looking out into the inky night.

'You ran away from home?' he said, his voice high and tight.

Her head snapped round and she glared at him. 'I did *not* run away from home. That's the sort of thing kids do! I'm an adult and I'm perfectly capable of making my own decisions, planning my own life...'

'Listen, I'm not one to judge—I've made plenty of the fall-off-a-cliff stupid decisions in my life. And I have to say, for a first attempt, yours was pretty spectacular.'

She frowned harder. 'How did you know it was my first attempt?'

His lips spread into a slow smile. 'Instinct.'

Allegra huffed and looked away again. 'You and your *instinct.* I just needed some time off, some space from all my commitments—I've been working like a dog since I turned sixteen—and it was about time I...' She trailed off and rested her chin on her knees.

'Oh, who am I kidding?' she snapped, then suddenly sat up again, dropped her knees to one side and turned to face him. 'Yes. I ran away from home. Okay?'

Finn couldn't help but smile at her. Who could have known the tiny mouse-like ballerina would turn out to be so fierce and fiery?

'It's not funny,' she said, taking in his smile. And then her mouth began to twitch. 'Really, it isn't.'

'What are you going to do?' he asked.

Allegra pulled her shoulders up to her ears and let them drop again. 'Don't know. I've put myself and the company in a rather unique position—there's no precedent for this. Dancers don't usually do a runner.' The corners of her mouth turned down. 'I could be out of a job.'

'A job you think you might hate,' Finn said softly. 'Maybe that's the silver lining?'

'But that's just it. I don't know if I do,' she replied despondently.

He watched the emotions play over her face in the warm orange torchlight. Even her face was exquisitely expressive. She didn't need to speak when she let the mask slip. He heard every thought. Every word.

'Then work it out,' he added. 'Dance. See if there's a spark left.'

She stared at the dark beach beyond the glow of their torches. 'Ugh. Enough of my problems. I came here to escape them.' She shook her head and then gave him a penetrating look. 'You know my entire life story now, but I hardly know anything about you. You know how I ended up a disgruntled ballerina. What journey did you take to become *Fearless Finn*—or did you just pop out of the womb that way?'

He laughed. 'Do *not* get my mother started on that subject!' Then he paused and thought a little. 'Not much to tell, really. Only child. Dad was in the forces, so I was an army brat and I travelled extensively when I was young. I'd always loved being outdoors, so climbing and hiking were natural interests for me, and with the constant changes of address there was always somewhere new to explore.'

Allegra stretched out and placed her hands behind her to support herself. The neatly crossed legs, with pointed feet, made Finn smile.

Her eyes softened. 'All that moving around. It must have been tough.'

'At first,' he said, nodding. 'But I got used to it.'

'Really?' she said, her brows pinching together. 'I don't think I could live like that. How did you cope?'

He grimaced. Lessons had been learned the hard way—dos and don'ts. Not a structured philosophy, more tips and tricks to survive the constant upheaval.

Don't get too attached to that best friend of yours, because he's going to have a face change in six months' time. Don't feed that stray cat that hangs around—and certainly don't fall in love with it—because we can't take it with us. Don't cry when you leave and don't look back. No point pining for what you can't have. Better to put all those sorts of feelings somewhere, fence them off and forget about them.

But *do* learn to make friends quickly. Always be cheerful. Always be fun to be with. Nobody wants to play with a sourpuss. Do get used to long distance phone calls and Christmases with relations you don't really remember. Do put down roots, if you really want to, but make sure they're shallow and they spread wide; that way you'll survive when they're ripped from the ground.

But Allegra didn't want to hear about all of that when she

was thousands of miles from home. It would only make her feel worse. So he shrugged lightly. 'Hide like an alligator, me. I must just be that type of person who thrives on change.'

Allegra shivered, and at first he thought it might be a re-action to what he'd said; but then he realised the temperature had dropped quite a bit since they'd left camp, the wind had picked up and, without the heat of the roaring fire he'd built, the air was starting to turn chilly. He stood and plucked a torch from the ground, then offered it to Allegra. He waited while she brushed the sand off her long, lean legs and then took the remaining torch for himself and led the way back to camp.

'What about after that?' Allegra asked as they fell into an easy stride.

Finn looked straight ahead. 'I joined the army when I was old enough. It was good for me—taught me how to channel my harem-scarem urges and put all the excess energy to good use.'

Allegra chuckled to herself as she watched where her feet were going. 'You mean you were *worse* back then? Lord help your poor mother! I don't think I would have liked to have met you as a teenage boy.'

No, thought Finn. Nor I you.

Because if he'd met a girl like this, a girl like Allegra, when he'd been a teenager, she'd have been very, very hard to leave behind.

He pushed the fanciful thought away and got back to hard facts. 'My army career took me all over the world, but I partic-ularly enjoyed learning how to survive in all of those places. There are so many skills we've forgotten now we've got our microwaves and cable TV and big sprawling cities. Somehow, by learning the skills that had been second nature to our an-cestors, I found a sense of...um...connection.'

This was easier territory now. He started to relax.

'I thought it would be a pity if all that expertise was lost to the modern world, so when I left the army I started up my own centre teaching survival skills. Then a couple of years ago Simon came on a team building weekend while he was still employed by a big TV company as an assistant working his way up the ranks. He came up with the basic idea for *Fearless Finn,* set up his own production company to make it when no one else was interested, and it just sort of went from there.'

They reached their camp and planted their torches in the sand. Close enough to give a bit of extra light, but not too close to the shelter. Allegra sat down on the log next to the fire pit, rested her forearms on her thighs and clasped her hands together.

'I see. So the TV programme came out of what you were doing already.'

He joined her on the log. 'I was very firm about the educational side of the programme. I only agreed to do it if it was going to be more than vicarious viewing. They're all very keen for me to do bonkers things, like eating weird insects or jumping into ice-cold water with next to nothing on. But while people are gasping at their TV screens they're hopefully learning something that could not just save but also enrich their lives.'

Allegra thought about that for a while. When she watched *Fearless Finn* on TV, he always seemed mind-bogglingly ready to jump into dangerous situations head first, but there was so much more to him than that. Why didn't he let people see that? It was odd, because he'd seemed so open and friendly right from the first moment she'd met him, and yet, even after almost four days together, constantly in each other's company, she was only just feeling as if she was starting to get to know him.

'You're really passionate about what you do, aren't you?' she said. 'It's not just about the adrenalin rush, is it?'

Finn's answering smile was softer and sadder than his

usual wide grin. 'I never pretended it was.' And he started
getting ready for the chill of the night, putting his shirt on
over his T-shirt, pulling his socks on over his feet once he'd
shaken the sand off, and then he climbed into the shelter.

No, he didn't pretend, thought Allegra. But he hid behind
other people's preconceptions of him just the same, and she'd
only just seen a hint of what lay behind it. She'd seen the
loneliness he'd been trying to hide when he'd talked about
his childhood, had sensed, just for a split second, that some
of that bravado was hollow.

And it was this knowledge that rang the death knell for
the teenage crush. Crushes were all about surface appeal, a
pretty canvas you could customise to meet your own fantasy.
Now she didn't care about the canvas at all. It was the man
underneath who had her spellbound, who tugged at her heart-
strings. And she hadn't thought this crazy situation could get
any worse.

She quickly got into the shelter and lay down. For some
reason she felt all shaky and her pulse was skipping along.

Stop it! she tried to tell her body. *You're wasting your energy. Save it for someone who's interested.*

But her pulse didn't listen; it just skipped all the harder.
She lay on her stomach, folded her hands on top of each other
and rested her chin on them. There. That would stop the quivering.

It had been nice while it had lasted, but it really was time
to face facts about Finn McLeod, wasn't it? She had to cut
this silly...*infatuation*...dead. And there was only one way
she could think of to start that process.

She tilted her head and looked at him. 'And what about
the future for Fearless Finn?'

Finn was lying on his back with his ankles crossed and
his hands tucked behind his head. He stared at the shelter
roof and made a tiny one-sided movement with his mouth. 'I

think the new format will secure the future of the show for at least another few years.'

Allegra smiled. 'I wasn't talking about the show. I was talking about you.' And then she looked away. 'You're getting married, aren't you?'

Finn didn't reply immediately, and the quivering spread from Allegra's hands up her arms and into her shoulders. She hoped the bamboo was lashed tightly enough not to jiggle. She knew she had to ask the next question, knew she had to stab her adolescent dreams in the heart. That would be her act of survival this week.

'What's she like? Nat?'

Finn went very still. When he answered he was staring at that palm thatching as if he could bore a hole through it. 'Dedicated. Ambitious. Driven. She understood not to cage me in. She let me be who I am.'

The quivering crept into Allegra's stomach and set up home there.

See? There was the problem. There was the reason she was all wrong for Finn McLeod.

If he was hers, she'd want to do exactly that—cage him in and keep him all for herself.

So now it was time to ask the question that really would knock the last nail in the coffin of her crush on Finn McLeod.

'So…how did you propose?'

She really didn't want to hear this. Knowing Finn, he'd have repelled out of a helicopter to surprise the lucky lady with a lump of diamond he'd carved from an African mine, or sky-written the question above her house—driving the plane himself, of course.

Finn coughed. 'You don't really want to know, do you?'

'Yes,' she replied. Maybe didn't want to know, but she *needed* to.

CHAPTER EIGHT

FINN cleared his throat. 'It was one of those rare periods when we were both in London together for more than a few days, and we were at my flat one evening, watching a documentary about dung beetles—'

Allegra almost choked on a laugh. 'Dung beetles?'

Finn ignored it. He didn't want to talk about this, but girls liked this kind of stuff, and Allegra wasn't to know that it had all been for nothing. Best thing was to give her the facts as quickly and cleanly as possible.

'Nat had just zoomed to the other side of town to pick up a few more of her things and when she got back she flopped down on the sofa beside me and said something about preferring downtown Kampala to London traffic these days. And then she said, "Maybe we should just move in together. It would save so much hassle."'

Allegra closed her eyes. Finn frowned but carried on.

'So I said, "Why don't we make it official, then?" and Nat thought about it for a minute and then said that was a good idea.'

'And then you went back to watching the dung beetles?'

'Yes,' Finn said, slightly puzzled. 'It was a very interesting programme.'

Allegra giggled loudly. What was wrong with her tonight?

'You old romantic,' she said, when she could finally speak again.

Finn folded his arms and scowled at her. 'Nat and I aren't the sort of people who need grand gestures.'

Well, he still didn't. Who knew about Nat any more? She'd certainly never been interested in chocolates and flowers when she'd been with him. And those sorts of things didn't come naturally to him. He'd never had the urge to do it spontaneously, so when he'd tried to be *romantic,* as Allegra put it, he'd had to plan and leave himself reminders. Even so, the gesture had always fallen flat when the vital moment had arrived.

He rolled onto his back again and folded his arms across his chest. 'I take it you like all of that nonsense?'

Allegra sighed, breathing out the last of her laughter. 'Yes. Now that I think about it, I think I do. So when my time comes for a proposal, I think I want a grand gesture. It's only supposed to happen once, so it might as well be spectacular.'

'Spoken like a true prima donna.'

Allegra pursed her mouth. He had a suspicion she was trying to stop herself from smiling. 'Prima donnas belong to the opera. I'm a ballet dancer.'

Finn just snorted. Allegra shook her head gently and then rolled onto her back. 'Sorry,' she said. 'I just thought that someone like you might have come up with something a little more...exciting.'

He rolled onto his side, facing away from her and muttered, 'Well, Nat didn't mind, so I don't see why you should.'

That sobered her up pretty quickly.

'No, no. You're right,' she said softly. 'I'm sorry. I'll shut up now.'

The silence that followed was definitely not comfortable and, as Finn's irritation cooled, he started to feel awful. He didn't know why he'd reacted so badly. Or why his ability to be friendly with everyone had suddenly deserted him. Maybe the whole Nat thing was getting to him finally.

He rolled over to look at Allegra. She'd turned her head to look at him, eyes glistening, but when he moved she quickly looked away.

He thought about Allegra, how contained she could be, how little she actually *said* about what she was feeling, even if he knew by reading her face. It had taken her a lot of guts to make that confession this evening. She deserved his honesty, too.

'Allegra?'

He thought he heard a tiny hiccup, and then she rolled her head to look at him.

'What?' she said quietly.

'I'm sorry,' he said. 'I didn't mean to snap at you. It's just it's a sore point at the moment, that's all.'

Her eyebrows lifted slightly and Finn took a deep breath.

'Nat asked me not to tell anyone yet, so I didn't really want to say anything…'

She propped herself up on her forearm and leaned forward a little. 'Finn?'

He shrugged with one shoulder. 'We broke up. We're not engaged any more. Her decision.'

A whole flurry of emotions passed across Allegra's features, none of which Finn could label because there were so many and they moved so fast.

'I'm sorry,' she said finally, and her voice was a little wobbly. 'Are you okay?'

This whole conversation was getting far too morose for Finn, far too close to that fenced off area of himself he tried not to think about, never mind go near. He decided to backtrack into safer territory. 'I'll survive,' he said jokingly and flashed her a grin.

She smiled back, but she was about as convincing as he'd been. 'Good.'

They both stared at each other. Finn felt he should say something, but his head was empty of words. In the end he cobbled something easy together.

'Goodnight, Allegra.'

She blinked. 'Goodnight, Finn.'

And then he rolled over and looked at the shelter wall. He daren't look back. There was something about those eyes of hers. Maybe she *was* a mermaid. Or a siren of some kind. Because sometimes, when he looked into them, he felt as if he was being sucked into their depths. And Finn McLeod didn't want to be sucked anywhere he couldn't escape from.

Allegra knew she ought to copy him and roll away, but she couldn't quite bring herself to do that. She was weak. She rolled onto the opposite side and stared at his back. Just a few minutes, she told herself, and then I'll turn over or close my eyes.

Forty minutes later she saw the movement of his ribs slow and soften as his breathing changed, indicating he'd drifted off to sleep.

Finn isn't getting married. He's free.

Those two sentences had been running round her head on a loop since he'd made the revelation.

Although the night was still and the sky clear tonight, she couldn't help thinking of him crouching by the edge of the shelter as the storm had raged above them on their first night. He'd seemed so energised. His face had practically glowed with excitement.

A very different picture from the Finn who had lain on his back, face expressionless, voice monotone, and had talked about the moment he'd asked the woman he was supposed to love to marry him.

She tried not to read anything into that, knowing it was probably all in her head—she was only seeing what she wanted to see—but she didn't have much success.

He's probably devastated underneath it all, she told herself. You can't let it mean anything. You can't pretend it changes anything.

How strange. Back home, the walls had been closing in on her and, try as she might, she hadn't been able to see a way out. There had been one, of course. She just hadn't had the courage to believe it was there, let alone take it. But this island had changed her already in strange and wonderful ways. Now, when her chances with Finn were slim to non-existent, she couldn't quite seem to shake the beautiful sense of hope that hung around her in the air.

Stupid girl.

Stupid mermaid.

Allegra woke early the following morning and her first semi-conscious thought was that she was late for something.

She had to get to class!

She scooted to the edge of the shelter and then she stopped moving, sat there in a daze with her legs dangling over the edge, wondering what on earth her body thought it was doing.

There was no daily ballet class here, remember? No reason to stretch and point and make her muscles work until they burned.

She missed it, she realised. She actually missed it.

Her body, which had been thrust into this alien environment full of unexpected challenges, suddenly longed for the familiarity of the barre, for the structure of a well taught class. She decided to run through her usual warm up stretches, just to ground herself.

She looked at Finn, still sleeping in the shelter, watched his chest rise and fall.

Had she dreamed what he'd said last night? Had she wished hard enough and made it true? He really wasn't getting married?

Don't be stupid, she told herself. Just because he isn't hers any more doesn't mean he's yours.

She made herself turn and walk a little farther away from the camp, keeping close to the treeline where the sand was flatter before it shelved down to the shore, and found a shady spot to exercise.

She started by rolling down her spine—oh, it was good— letting each vertebra curl and stretch as she kept her pelvis upright and let her arms dangle down towards her toes. When she reached the bottom she just hung there for a few seconds, letting her arms get heavy, enjoying the gentle pull in the backs of her legs. Then she rolled back up again and repeated the movement a few more times. If her body could have talked it would have let out a contented sigh. So she moved from one stretch to the next to the next…

'I didn't think it was possible for a human body to do that.'

Allegra let go of her leg, the calf of which had been gently nudging her ear, and whipped her head round. She had one hand resting lightly on the bark of a palm tree for balance. Just as well, really, if Finn McLeod was going to sneak up on her like that.

The leg stayed where it was for a second or so and she let it move towards the ground slowly, maintaining control over every muscle until her toes touched the sand.

'You're right,' she said, trying not to feel as if she'd been caught red-handed. 'A human body isn't supposed to do that. However, every choreographer I've ever worked with has paid little attention to what's physically possible. Sometimes us dancers have to work out a way to do it anyway.'

Finn's look of awe was replaced by his customary grin. 'It'd be a bloody miracle if I could get my leg to do that!'

The mental image conjured up by Finn's outburst tickled Allegra greatly. Although she knew the male dancers she worked with were as strong as any Olympic athlete, somehow the thought of Finn doing ballet was all *wrong.* He had this energy about him—this untameable, masculine, raw energy—that ballet would never be able to contain.

On the other hand, if Finn ever gave up adventuring and decided to become the next Patrick Swayze, there'd be a global stampede of women wanting to be his partner.

She flushed hot at the thought herself, and quickly buried her face in her knees in a pretend hamstring stretch to hide it. When she pulled herself upright again she found Finn sitting cross-legged on the sand looking expectant.

'What?' she said.

Finn looked innocent. Well, as innocent as a man with a devil-may-care twinkle in his eye could. 'I was hoping all that elasticity was preparation for a display, that maybe you were going to dance. I wanted to see if I could tell if you still loved it or not.'

Allegra crossed her arms over her torso and hugged her own waist. 'Oh, no,' she said. 'I don't think I'm ready for that yet.'

Though the playful tone in his voice remained, a hint of seriousness darkened his eyes. 'There's only one way to find out, you know.'

She knew.

But she really wasn't ready. Wasn't ready to discover if, when she left this island—and Finn—behind, the only constant in her life wouldn't be waiting for her when she got home.

That, and the fact she *really* didn't want Finn to see her dance.

She walked over to where he was and gracefully folded her legs under herself until she was sitting beside him. Not too close, mind you.

'I know,' she said carefully, trying to scrunch up her toes so he wouldn't see how ugly her art had made them. 'Maybe tomorrow.'

She couldn't let him see her dance. It would be far too dangerous, far too revealing. It wouldn't have mattered a couple of weeks ago, because she'd have had nothing to hide then— but now... Now she felt as if every emotion she'd been holding in check would come seeping out of her pores as soon as she began to move.

Then he'd know.

And, as hopeful as the mermaid part of her had been last night under a starlit sky, the practical ballerina, bathed in morning light, knew better, knew she was asking for too much.

'Okay,' said Finn, clapping his hands and hoisting himself up. 'If no gala performance is forthcoming, I think it's high time you worked on your fire skills.'

Allegra groaned out loud. Despite her best efforts, that particular talent still eluded her. But, as frustrating as another attempt would be, she'd do it because it was a safe activity and, where Finn McLeod was concerned, safe was definitely good.

The fresh young coconuts at the top of the palm tree were taunting him. He looked up at them, dangling out of reach on the tree that he'd picked out as the most scalable near their camp.

'Why can't we just grab one off the beach again?' Allegra asked. 'They're all over the place.'

'Not the same,' Finn muttered, eyes still fixed on the large green nuts sitting under the palm leaves at the top of the tree. 'Coconuts that have fallen off the tree are mature. The flesh is drier and they have much less liquid.'

And he had a hankering for the gelatinous sweetness he knew the young nuts contained. A hankering he was allowing to overtake the sensible side of his brain—the side that kept reminding him he was expending *way* more energy harvesting the food than he would gain in calories from eating it—

because focusing on *this* craving was a very nice distraction from other things he shouldn't be hankering for.

He had another go. The bottom of the trunk ran at forty-five degrees to the ground for about eight feet and then it rose proudly upwards for another twenty. He jumped on, walked up the first part, using his hands for leverage, then changed technique when the trunk became vertical. He'd seen locals on more tropical islands than he cared to count doing something similar. Kids, even! Surely it couldn't be that hard?

After two frog-like jumps up the tree, he lost his grip and came crashing down on the sand, narrowly avoiding a face-plant.

Dave roared with laughter and zoomed in on him. Finn simmered inside. He was almost certain that one would end up in an out-takes show at some point in the near future. He was tempted to vent his frustration, just so they could add a few of the obligatory bleepings-out, but he managed to contain himself. Just.

He rolled over onto his back and looked up at the sky. At the fringes of his vision he could see Allegra, hands on hips, her ponytail swaying as she guffawed behind her hand.

'It's not funny,' he said, pulling himself up. 'It takes a great deal of strength, balance and coordination to pull that off. I'd like to see you try.'

It had been a throwaway comment, but she stopped laughing and arched an eyebrow at him. 'Things I've been told I have plenty of,' she said.

The crew went very quiet, which was normally a sign he was about to do something totally stupid, or they were aware something really filmable was about to happen.

Funnily enough, he didn't want Allegra to be joining him on that out-takes show.

'Really? You want to try?' He looked at the tree again, carefully scanning every inch from the bottom to the top. 'I'm telling you, falling on this sand is like falling on concrete.'

'Don't you think I can do it?'

He met her gaze. Instead of the doubt and fear he might have seen there a few days ago, he saw a spark of defiance, a challenge. It made her even more appealing.

He looked back at the tree again. Nothing appealing about that awkward bit of vegetation, so he was safe there.

'Be my guest,' he said, expecting Tim, the safety expert, to veto him. But Tim just nodded and waved towards the tree.

'Consider putting on your long-sleeved shirt,' Finn added, pulling himself up off the ground. 'It might save you some scraped arms.'

Allegra glanced over at the shelter, which was maybe thirty feet away, and then shook her head. 'I'll risk it,' she said, and walked over to the bottom of the tree.

Part of Finn wanted to tell her to go and get it anyway. The other part was pleased she was finally listening to her gut. It meant she might have a chance of surviving the surprise final challenge after all.

Allegra must have seen him try to shimmy up that tree at least twenty times this morning, and she copied his moves perfectly. More than perfectly, actually, because she walked up the tree and got into the froggie position easily. Then she pressed down with her feet and jumped upwards, hugging the trunk lightly with both arms. A couple more times and she stopped.

Finn's heart began to hammer. That was the bit where he always fell off. But she turned her head to grin at all of them on the ground and then carried on. That was when she really found her rhythm. She shot up that tree like a monkey, those long, flexible legs and hardened feet making short work of it. Once again, Finn thought that if learning ballet gave you strength like that, he just might have to take it up himself.

Only if he didn't have to wear tights, of course.

'How many do you want?' she called from the top of the tree.

'Two or three,' he yelled back. 'Twist them. They should come down fairly—'

He jumped out of the way of a plummeting coconut that had threatened to turn his bare toes to mush.

Amazing. Just like those kids who could shimmy up those trees in no time. Her smaller, lighter frame was much more suited to coconut tree climbing than his.

Another coconut thudded to the ground. And then another, which rolled lazily towards him. He bent down and picked it up. Then he walked over to a low rock a little further down the beach and set about opening it up with his machete. Hopefully, by the time she was back down on the ground he'd have it ready and waiting for her.

'Finn?' She sounded a little nervous.

He glanced back at the tree, where she was still half-hidden under the bushy palm leaves that clustered at the top. He left the machete embedded in the coconut shell and stood up. 'Yeah?'

'Erm…how do I get down again?' she yelled. 'I'm afraid I haven't seen you do it any way I'd like to copy.'

That was when the silent crew blew it by hooting with laughter. He would have got cross with them if they'd been laughing at her, but they weren't. The joke was on him.

He walked towards the tree, shielding his eyes with the flat of his hand, but before he'd opened his mouth to offer some advice, she started to reverse the climbing process. She made it back down just as successfully, if a little more slowly and clumsily, and then jumped to the ground when she was close enough. No ungainly thudding as he would have done. Her legs bent deeply and she kept her back beautifully straight. She made so little noise he suspected there might not even be a dent in the sand where she landed.

'I'll make sure I bring you with me on my next desert island trip,' he said cheerily, and then wondered why he'd ever let those words out of his mouth.

The smile of accomplishment that had lit up Allegra's features disappeared. The camera crew went quiet again. She looked away.

'No, you won't,' she said. 'This is a one-time deal. We both know that.'

He knew that. In a couple of days she'd go back to her life and he'd go back to his. He just hadn't realised how much he didn't want to believe that, or how empty the prospect made him feel. He wanted to do the whole series with her, to take her to every new place and see her eyes sparkle at each new wonder. And there was a whole planet to explore. They could keep going for ever.

If this weren't a one-time deal...

He kicked one of the fallen coconuts with his bare foot. Bad idea. And then he walked back to the one he'd cracked open, hiding his limp as best he could. Didn't work. The crew started snickering again.

'Where's the brown hairy bit?' Allegra said from over his shoulder as he made several deep cuts into the end of the green shell.

'Ah,' he said. 'You'll see.' With the final slice of the knife he spotted a small dark hole in the glistening white flesh. He stood up and held the coconut up to her lips. 'Try it.'

Her hands came up to steady it and he carefully moved his fingers so they didn't brush hers. Afterwards he realised they wouldn't have done anyway, because she'd been equally as careful about not touching his. He ignored that thought. Didn't want to consider what it might mean.

When she had it steady in her hands, he let go entirely and stepped back.

There. Much safer.

She tipped her head back and the coconut with it. The clear juice ran out, taking her by surprise. She caught most of it, but some ran out of her mouth and down her chin. Finn licked his lips.

She held the coconut in one hand and, laughing, wiped her chin with the back of the other one.

'Do you want some?' She held the bright green shell out to him.

Finn didn't move. Couldn't. He feared if he did he might do something monumentally stupid. Not just falling-off-a-cliff stupid, but end-of-the-world-as-we-know-it stupid.

A small drip of coconut water was hanging on Allegra's bottom lip and he watched it, stomach muscles tightening, as it hugged the rounded fullness and then dribbled down her chin. He couldn't take his eyes off that drip.

Allegra stopped laughing and hugged the coconut to her abdomen. He managed to unhook his gaze from her lips for a second and flick it to her eyes. She was looking at him with a startled expression.

They stayed like that for a few long seconds. Allegra was the first one to break eye contact, but her gaze didn't drift far. Only downwards an inch or so. He felt his mouth dry and as he was about to moisten it Allegra mirrored him by running the tip of her tongue across her bottom lip.

The sound of the wind in the palm branches above their heads disappeared. The surf must have paused itself, because he didn't hear a single wave crash. But in the flawless silence he heard the shallow rasp of her breath, the pounding of his blood in his ears.

He was staring at her mouth, and she was staring at his. They both seemed to realise this in the same instant and shifted their gaze to look into each other's eyes.

Finn felt something slam into his chest. At first he thought it was another coconut falling from the tree, but when searing pain didn't follow he realised it was something else. It wasn't a solid object that had almost knocked him off his feet but a realisation.

Whatever strange magnetic forces on this island had caused him to lose his mind in the last twenty four hours— she was feeling them, too.

Dave coughed, and that simple, basic human noise cracked the bubble of silence that had surrounded her and Finn. Now that there was air, Allegra sucked some in then thrust the green coconut at Finn's chest before stepping away. His hands came up to grip it out of sheer reflex. He didn't look away.

Then, suddenly, it was all over, and movement and noise and sensation returned. The crew sprang into action as Finn fetched one of the bamboo cups he'd made and poured the rest of the coconut water into it. Dave and the other cameraman moved in close to get the best angles as Finn picked up his machete and set about splitting the coconut with unusual vigour, even for him. Allegra quietly backed away and let them all swarm in.

She'd seen what she'd thought she'd seen, hadn't she? Or had it just been more wishful thinking? Mermaid thinking?

He'd finished opening up the coconut now and he used his knife to split the husk and carve two wedge-shaped spoons from the green shell. Dave and the other crew drew back as Finn offered her one. She felt she had no choice but to walk down the path they'd created for her. She moved slowly and carefully, her bare feet working through from toe to heel, as if she were walking onto a stage.

She took the spoon, once again careful not to make contact, and crouched down beside the rock he was carving the coconut on. Neither of them looked at anything but the coconut.

She scraped her spoon into the snowy-white coconut innards and was surprised when instead of meeting dense, hard flesh the piece of shell sank in and she was able to easily scoop out what looked like slightly unset yoghurt. Finn did likewise and instantly wolfed it down, letting his eyelids close

lightly as he savoured the taste. Allegra didn't move. Not because she didn't want to eat, but because the message hadn't
quite travelled from brain to arm yet. But when Finn swallowed and she sensed he was going to open his eyes again
she focused fiercely on her spoon.

Now that she had coconut-related visual stimulation her
arm jerked to life and she lifted the spoon to her lips.

It was like…

She didn't know what it was like. The texture was inde-
scribable, but it tasted like coconut she'd had before only more
delicate and sweeter and—this sounded quite strange—more
alive. She knew why Finn had closed his eyes now, because
she could hardly resist doing the same herself.

When she'd finished the first mouthful she reached her
spoon out to gather a second, and made the mistake of catching Finn's eye as she did so.

Clunk.

It happened again. Their gazes snagged like Velcro.

He'd been watching her, watching her reaction to her first
taste of sweet young coconut. He'd just had some himself, yet
he looked like a starving man.

She swallowed, even though her spoon and her mouth remained empty.

She hadn't been imagining it. Not one bit. And that knowledge flipped everything on its head, because now she wasn't
longing for the impossible any more. A door of opportunity
had been opened for her.

But was she stupid enough—and brave enough—to walk
through it?

CHAPTER NINE

Allegra did nothing. At least, she *said* nothing. Maybe that meant she was still a coward, that all that shouting and screaming and *letting it all out* on the hilltop had been nothing more than a good way to make her tonsils sore. She couldn't seem to bring any of that liberty to her tongue now, as she worked and ate and slept next to Finn.

Only two more nights. Time was running out now.

She was at the far end of the beach, on a food gathering task Finn had set for her. It was safe enough now to turn and look. She could see his khaki shape moving around near their shelter.

She sighed and turned back to the ocean. *Bring back something edible,* Finn had said. Allegra had avoided the crabs that scuttled near the rock pools—not much chance of getting them back to camp with all her digits intact. She'd also spotted a conch shell further along in the shallows, but it was probably empty. She'd already gathered some squashy, succulent leaves of sea purslane, but she decided to check the shell out anyway.

She placed the tropical salad she'd gathered onto the wet sand before wading into the shallows to inspect the conch. It was horrendously heavy, which gave her hope, but when she upended it she discovered a shiny pink interior. Premises vacated. Just a pretty shell with nothing inside.

Like her, really. Big on appearances, not so hot on the following through.

She'd had all these great plans of how she was going to tell Finn she was attracted to him, and they had all come to nothing. She'd rehearsed a hundred speeches—from flirty and cheeky to deep and meaningful—fully intending to deliver them, but when an opportunity came, she clammed up and the moment passed.

She really was a mute little mermaid, wasn't she? And had just as much luck with the men.

She dropped the shell back into the water and waded back to shore, where she gathered up the purslane and headed back to camp to show Finn her find.

'Great,' he said, only half looking up from the fire. 'Want to help me prepare the meal?'

She nodded, and they worked side by side in silence, passing tools, taking turns to check the fish roasting there on a stick.

Must be really riveting TV, she thought, as she bit into some sea purslane and savoured its saltiness. The crew had been fidgety for a day or so now. Probably because she and Finn had tacitly settled into a rhythm with each other. They worked as a team, saying only what needed to be said to get the jobs done. All the other words were kept under lock and key.

And, even though the cameras and microphones were high-tech and very sensitive, Allegra was glad they hadn't yet invented a recording device that could capture what was humming between her and Finn. They didn't even have to look at each other now to feel it. It was there from the moment they opened their eyes in the morning until their brains succumbed to unconsciousness at night. And probably in between.

Not just a physical awareness—it had gone long past that—but a sense of completeness, a profound sense of connection.

And she knew she wasn't alone in feeling it. At least, her mermaid brain told her she wasn't alone, and she was inclined to believe it.

For the first time in her life, Allegra felt as if she'd not only met someone's expectations, but exceeded them. And it was sweetness to her soul.

The air was oppressive. Every molecule seemed to be humming. Even under the canopy of dense vegetation in the island's interior, Finn didn't need to look up to know that clouds had blocked out the sun.

'We need to get a move on,' he yelled over his shoulder. A rumble of thunder out at sea backed him up.

The crew fell silent and picked up speed. Simon called for the speedboat on his satellite phone. It would have been another fifteen minutes before they'd be back on the beach, and if this storm was as bad as the last one, the crew needed to make a quick escape. The rain could last for hours and they were too close to sunset to wait it out. And there was no way all five of them would squish into his and Allegra's tiny shelter. If the crew stayed, someone was going to get wet—and that someone would probably be him.

Thankfully, although the charge in the air increased, those rumbles remained distant, for now at least.

When they finally reached the camp the pace became even more frantic as Tim, Dave, Barry and Simon ran around gathering up kit. He and Allegra, meanwhile, started hauling their stack of firewood towards the shelter. They shoved as much as they could underneath the raised sleeping platform to keep it dry. The crew helped them until the boat turned up and then they waved a hasty goodbye and disappeared round the headland in their tiny white boat.

Just in time, it seemed, because a few minutes later it began to rain.

Allegra didn't need to be told to jump into the shelter. Neither did he.

But once inside he encountered a bit of a problem.

While they'd been preparing for the rain, he'd been fine. He'd kept himself busy, had fallen back on his training. Training that was the culmination of generations of experience, passed down from ancestor to ancestor. Finn was proud to be a modern-day keeper of this diminishing knowledge. It made him feel not just connected to nature but connected to the past, connected to humanity.

But now, as the rain began to fall, he had nothing left to do but sit it out. No job to distract him. And when it came to coping with what he was starting to feel for the woman he was sharing a tiny bamboo and palm leaf shelter with, he had no knowledge base, no ancient wisdom to fall back on. In this situation he was totally on his own.

Help.

Uncharted territory. Not something he was normally afraid of. But there was always a first time for everything.

The wind picked up, ruffling the frilly green thatching on the shelter roof. Another rumble. Longer this time. Closer.

He and Allegra stopped looking out at the grey sky and the dirty blue sea and looked at each other instead.

There was connection. Looking back at him with bright blue eyes.

Not connection to ancient wisdom, or long-dead people. No, connection to a living, breathing person, who was mere inches away from him.

He always told his survival students that if they were ever stuck in a jungle they shouldn't be tempted to stay any longer than necessary. *Get out,* he told them. *And get out fast.* It was what he wanted to do right now.

Run, a voice in his head was telling him. Run as fast as you can. Don't stop. Don't even look back. This is not a place to get entangled or put down roots. It's dangerous terrain, remember? That was why he'd mentally fenced it off and declared it 'out of bounds' years ago.

Seemed as though he was lost, though. Or stuck in quicksand. Because he couldn't even look away, let alone move his legs.

He held his breath, waiting for a lightning bolt that was long overdue, yet still refused to come.

The storm seemed to have stolen their voices. Neither of them had uttered a word to each other since the crew had left. But words weren't really needed. They would only say what they were *supposed* to say, skirt around the thing staring them both in the face. The communication going on between them now was much more honest.

She was just as lost as he was. Just as stuck. He saw it in her eyes. Saw the questions flit across them, saw the answers he'd given, without realising, register and hit home.

And suddenly he didn't want to run any more. If he was lost, he didn't want to be found. He wanted to turn around, peer inside those forbidden boundaries and see what was inside.

That was when it happened—when the searing flash of light split the sky and made the air tremble. In that second, when his eyes were dancing with colour and the audible release of power was still echoing in his ears, Finn took his first step.

They were kneeling opposite each other and, slowly, he leaned forward and reached for her with one hand. He didn't drag her to him instantly, but traced her jaw with his thumb, her long neck with his fingers. Warmth upon warmth. Skin upon skin. Her pulse rapid beneath his palm.

No mad skydive into the unknown this time for Finn McLeod. He was taking his time, feeling his way. Savouring every sensation.

Allegra hadn't blinked since he'd touched her, but now her lids slid closed and her head tipped back.

Finn found the soft skin between collarbone and chin with his lips, not really sure how he'd moved closer. He didn't care, didn't stop to analyse how or why. He was too lost in tasting her, exploring her, working ever so slowly upwards, feeling her melt against him further with each kiss.

She grabbed onto him for support, sinking her long fingers into his unruly hair, holding him prisoner, making it impossible for him to pull away. But he didn't feel trapped. It only increased the heat building inside of him.

And when his mouth neared the end of its upward climb and crested the curve of her jaw they both paused. His hands were either side of her head, hers on his neck and shoulder. For a few seconds they hovered there, eyes closed, breathing shallow and ragged, lips only millimetres apart.

Finn had always wondered if a daring leap or a foolish stunt would eventually be his undoing. How ironic that, in the end, it turned out to be the tiniest of movements, the sweetest and softest of kisses that sealed his fate.

Every cell in Allegra's body seemed to be singing, bursting with life and joy.

It was better than she'd imagined. Way better than the tightly wrapped girlish fantasies: big on longing, a little fuzzy on detail. Finn brought that wildness, that dizzying sense of rawness to his kisses.

Oh, it had started off soft and light, but it hadn't stayed that way for long. Quickly, the overwhelming force between them had dragged them down and pulled them under. So completely lost in the moment was she that she couldn't even form a coherent thought. She couldn't remember where his lips had been last or guess where his fingers might touch next. Finally, she'd reached that place where instinct reigned and, boy, was there spark to go with it.

She shivered, and she wasn't sure if it was in response to the drop in air temperature caused by the storm or a reaction to Finn's lips on hers, his tongue gently sending her over the edge. Finn felt her body shudder, too, and his arms came round her to steady her, then slowly, slowly he pulled away.

Even kneeling he was so much taller than her and she tipped her head to look up at him as he smoothed her hair out of her face and looked deep into her eyes.

She couldn't help it—she smiled. Beamed at him.

Finn smiled back, but it wasn't his usual ready-for-anything grin, and Allegra knew she was seeing that part of him he rarely revealed to others. She saw it all—the little boy who'd been uprooted so many times, yet had still worked out a way to survive, the teenager who had substituted the glory of nature and adrenalin rushes for more tricky human relationships. And she loved everything she saw. It only bound her to him more deeply.

Tread gently. Softly.

Something told her in this, despite her own inexperience, she would need to be his guide, his teacher. If he'd let her.

She reached up and touched her lips to his. Told him so without words.

He responded by pulling her against him, holding her there with a fierce protectiveness. If only, she thought. If only he'd always want to keep me like this, close to him, safe by his side. She felt she could do anything, conquer every challenge if he were beside her.

Lightning flashed again, followed a few seconds later by growling thunder. Loud still, but the storm was passing by quickly. In unison, they glanced outside. A flash of metallic silver in one of the trees opposite made them both pause.

Oh, no. She'd totally forgotten about the non-native technology hidden in the foliage. Had it been dark enough for the night vision camera to capture what had just been going on? Euphoria gave way to panic.

She looked at Finn and found him eyeing the camera suspiciously, too.

She shivered. They'd been away from the camp for quite some time this afternoon and the fire had just been glowing embers when they'd got back. No chance of starting one in this downpour. Not until the rain stopped and they could use the wood that they'd stacked under their shelter.

Another shiver rattled her shoulders.

Finn released her and sat down, then opened his arms. She didn't ask what he was offering, just turned round and scooted back into him, letting his torso warm her back as his arms closed lightly around her. They sat like that, watching the rain, saying nothing.

Darkness fell. The thunder and lightning rumbled away but the rain continued. Finn shifted, and she knew somehow that was her signal to crawl out of his arms. The damp breeze instantly found the gap between their bodies as she moved away, puckering the skin on her back into gooseflesh.

Finn changed position. He gently eased himself down onto his side, ready for sleep. But not facing away from her. She accepted his subtle invitation and matched his pose, tucking her much shorter form against his. She could feel his breath at the back of her ear as his warm arm came around her to steady them both.

He didn't stroke. He didn't caress. He didn't do anything he shouldn't have. Just kept her warm.

Don't hope for too much, remember? Only mermaids hope. And when that hope dies they dissolve into nothing, like the foam on the sea.

She tried to be sensible, tried to tell herself not to hope, but it wasn't easy with Finn wrapped around her, the thump of his heart marking her back.

Finn woke to find himself still curled around Allegra. From the grey tinge to the sky, he could tell it was just before dawn. The rain had finally stopped.

He'd never slept like this with Nat. Somebody's knees or

elbows had inevitably got in someone else's way, and one or both of them would have ended up moving apart, needing their own space.

He should move. He needed to start a fire. Neither of them had eaten the evening before, but it seemed a crime to pull away. They fitted. Too well, maybe.

He would move in a minute. He would.

This was his last chance to be alone with her, his last chance to consider exploring the uncharted areas of his soul that he hadn't realised had existed until a tiny ballerina had thrown herself out of a helicopter at him and knocked them both to the ground.

Had that really been less than seven days ago? Was there really little more than twenty-four hours left before the speed-boat arrived one last time and whisked them away?

Yes.

That meant he had precious little time to daydream and think about himself. He would get Allegra breakfast, because she would need all the strength she could get if she was going to make it through her final day on the island. Her final night, too.

Reluctantly, he lifted the arm that had been holding her against him, shuffled backwards a little and waited. She frowned in her sleep, but didn't wake. Finn sat up and stared at her. Marvelled at how something that seemed so fragile and delicate could be so strong.

And he missed her as he edged away and began to rebuild their fire.

Missed her more than he wanted to, and more than he should have. Maybe because, although Allegra didn't know this yet, they had just shared their last night together on the island.

Finn looked up from where he was crouching over the fire and handed her a scorched bit of fish. Allegra took it gratefully. Even though they'd had breakfast, no dinner the night before meant her stomach still felt as if it was rubbing against her backbone. Lunch was very, very welcome.

She tried to catch Finn's eye before he returned his attention to the fire, but he didn't even make eye contact.

She pulled the blackened, crunchy skin off the bit of fish and sank her teeth into the succulent white flesh, eyes still on him.

The crew had been unpacking when she'd woken alone in the shelter that morning. She'd had no opportunity to be on her own with Finn, let alone talk to him since then. The cameras had started rolling and he'd hardly even looked at her.

The fish, which she'd really been looking forward to, suddenly was as appealing as wet cardboard. She wanted to spit it out on the sand.

He was being like this because of the cameras, right? Merely being discreet. She hoped desperately that was the case. The alternative was that she'd just become the latest addition to his list of falling-off-a-cliff mistakes and that he was too embarrassed to look at her.

She swallowed the lump of fish with difficulty and took another bite. Tasteless.

But then Finn turned to offer her some more and this time something flashed between them, as hot and bright and pure as the lightning from the night before. A look full of meaning. A look that made Allegra's stomach muscles unclench and her pulse race.

It *was* for the cameras.

And, now she wasn't panicking about it, she could see that being discreet made sense. After all, the rest of the world still believed he was a soon-to-be married man. But even if that hadn't been the case, she could imagine that Finn would have veered away from public displays of affection, however passionate he might be in private. She stepped closer to the fire, grateful she could use it to excuse the bright flush of her cheeks.

Time to play Finn's game and play it well. Nothing was going on between them. Nothing at all.

She glanced over at Barry, the second cameraman. 'Where's Dave today?' she asked when she'd finished her mouthful, even though she knew she was supposed to ignore them as much as possible. She'd kind of got used to Dave's burly, if slightly grouchy, presence.

Barry shrugged the shoulder that wasn't balancing a camera. 'Got something else to do,' he mumbled.

Chatty, Allegra thought. She hesitated a second before she spoke to Finn, but she decided he was the one person she was supposed to interact with on a regular basis, so it wouldn't look out of place if she asked him a question. All she had to do was keep the longing out of her eyes. Surely, she could manage that for a few seconds?

She turned to him, schooling her facial muscles into a neutral state. 'So what hoops are you going to make me jump through today, Fearless Finn?'

Was it just her imagination or did the entire crew pause for a split second?

Finn messed around poking the fire with a stick for a few seconds. When he lifted his head to look at her there was something different about his eyes. It was as if a door had been shut and she couldn't see all the way into them any more. Just more acting, right? He was getting rather good at it.

'If we really were stranded on this island,' he said, 'we'd want to find a way to get off it.'

She nodded, ever the good student.

'Making a signal fire to alert passing ships to our presence would be one of our aims,' he added.

Fire? Yippee. Her favourite game.

'On the beach here?' she asked.

Finn shook his head. 'The old ruin on the tip of the island

would be a better spot. If that really was a fort or a lookout post of some sort, it would give us a clue that local shipping patterns might bring boats closer to that point.'

'Okay.'

She didn't really care what she did today as long as she got to spend every minute of it with him. She'd even build a giant fire and dance around it for him if he wanted her to.

'Right,' Finn said, and stood up. 'We'd better start packing up our stuff.'

'Packing?'

Finn walked over to the shelter and started stuffing things into his backpack, which had been tucked just inside the entrance. 'We would have only minutes to light the fire if we saw a ship,' he said as he picked his machete up and slipped it into the holder on his leg. 'There's no point being over an hour's walk away. The best place to set up camp tonight is in the ruins.'

Allegra followed him, smiling and shaking her head. Finn stopped what he was doing and smiled back at her. 'What?'

They both had their backs to the crew, who weren't really paying them any attention. It was the closest they'd had to privacy all day.

'I can't believe I'm going to miss this old shelter,' she said quietly, giving one of the upright poles an affectionate pat.

Finn didn't say anything, he just carried on packing. But as he searched the leafy jungle mattress for forgotten essentials, he glanced around and caught her eye and gave her another one of those scorching looks.

Me, too, his eyes said. And not just that.

They said it so beautifully that she wanted to stop him, place a palm on either side of his face and kiss her agreement.

She didn't, of course. She picked up her long-sleeved shirt and put it on. Once her boots were laced up, that was her ready. They finished their packing silently, the familiar thrumming feeling joining them, no matter where they moved around camp, so they were always aware of one another. They didn't have much to pack, really, and it was only ten minutes before they were heading off towards the old ruins.

On the way there Finn became unusually obsessed with navigational techniques. 'We're heading north. Remember that,' he kept saying, and then he'd repeat once again all the ways a lost adventurer could keep on track if they weren't in possession of a compass.

Allegra was only half listening. She had more important work to do. Most of the time she wasn't even paying attention to what direction she was going. She was, however, definitely paying a lot of attention to Finn—saving up little details for the scrapbook of memories from her magical week on a desert island with the most amazing man she'd ever met.

Silly things. Little things.

The way he moved: always direct, always efficient, never dithering or meandering, whether he was striding through the forest or reaching for his knife.

The angle of his jaw and cheekbone as he turned to point something out to her, which he did countless times each day. She wanted a mental snapshot of that, for sure.

His smile. The pitch of his laugh, deep brown like his eyes. The exact way his delicious accent curled around certain words.

Little things, yes. But important things.

They'd been going for about forty-five minutes when Finn suddenly stopped. Allegra almost bumped into the back of him. He held out a hand—low, slightly behind him, palm down—and they all stopped and fell silent.

'What is it?' Tim asked from behind, ever on the lookout for danger. He moved past Allegra to stand beside Finn, who had crept forward a couple of paces. They chatted in hushed tones for a few moments and then Finn looked over his shoulder and gave her a smile that didn't even attempt to make it all the way to his eyes.

'Just stay there for a second,' he said firmly.

She watched as the men headed farther up the trail. Well, Finn said it was a trail and she believed him. To Allegra, one bit of the jungle looked very much like the next. Just before their khaki clothes made them disappear into the greenery, Finn headed back in her direction, looking very serious indeed. Allegra's heart began to thud.

'What?' she said in a tight voice when he reached her.

Warmth slid into Finn's fierce gaze. 'It's up to you now,' he said. 'Until sunrise tomorrow. This is your last challenge. You can do it.'

And then he shrugged his backpack off and thrust it towards her. She gripped onto it and hugged it to her chest. Finn turned as if to walk away and Allegra opened her mouth to ask what he meant, but her question died as he did an about face and pressed a hot, quick kiss to her lips before running off into the jungle.

Up to her? What did that mean? Did he mean she was going to have to build the fire on her own? They'd be stranded here for ever if that was the case. Mind you, maybe that wasn't such a bad idea...

The bird calls and other noises seemed to have got suddenly louder, and she held her breath at every rustling leaf and cracking twig—things she had never done when Finn had been around. At least Simon was here to keep her company.

She peered into the dense green foliage ahead. Something moved near her feet and she froze, trying desperately to remember what Finn had told her about snakes. Were you supposed to stamp around making a noise, or were you supposed to go as quietly as you could? Perhaps Simon would know. She turned round to ask him.

That was when she got her second shock of the morning.

He wasn't there.

Not a sound to indicate where he'd gone or even a swaying branch to show which route he'd taken.

Sweat was dripping between Allegra's shoulder blades.
Her shirt was damp and her hair was sticking to her head.
Even so, she shivered.

What was she going to do?

She was in the middle of a jungle, thousands of miles from
home, and she was totally and utterly alone.

CHAPTER TEN

IF THERE had been anywhere to sit down, she would have sat down. But one thing she'd learned from Finn about terrain like this was never to put anything down on an uncleared bit of ground—especially a body part you didn't want teeth or fang marks in.

So she stood, and she waited.

It took more than five minutes before she let the meaning of Finn's last words even *start* to sink in. She swung round, keeping her feet planted, hoping to see something other than multilayered shades of green that stretched on for as far as the eye could see. Then she hugged the rucksack tighter and turned slowly on her heels.

What had Finn drummed into her? In this kind of environment you've got to slow down, stay calm. The worst thing she could do was panic.

She stopped turning and stared straight ahead. Uh-oh. She had already broken that rule. Turning round had been a bad idea. She wasn't facing the same way she had been a few moments ago, and now she didn't know which way the ruins were.

Her pulse started to jog.

How do you know that? How do you know you're not facing the right direction? It all looks the same, this green stuff, doesn't it?

An image flashed into her mind—Finn and Tim stepping over the slim brown trunk of a fallen tree. They'd still been heading north. She needed to follow the same trail.

She turned again, more slowly this time, until she spotted something like it. Yes, that was definitely it. Then she tipped her head back, looking for the sun.

Head north.

It had to be early afternoon still, which meant she should keep the sun on her…left. Okay. She could do this. She'd follow the path she thought Finn and Tim had taken, and she'd use all the tips Finn had given her on the way. The ones she remembered, anyway. But she was right about the sun, she knew that much.

By conscious decision, she relaxed her arm muscles and loosened her grip on the rucksack, then she slung the straps over her shoulders and adjusted them before looking straight ahead.

Only another ten minutes or so until she reached the fort. She could manage that without getting lost, couldn't she?

Allegra drew a deep breath in through her nostrils and began to walk.

It was closer to twenty minutes before the dense vegetation thinned and she could see the sea sparkling through the trees and bushes. She let out a long breath as she pushed her way through the last twenty feet and out onto a small beach. She must have been slightly off course, because she'd been aiming for the northern tip of the island. However, she kept the sun on the correct side and after a few minutes she realised her destination was straight ahead and then off to the left. This was the beach that ran down the eastern side of the island's tip.

She'd done it!

Smiling, she climbed up the rocks at the edge of the beach until she reached the grassy plateau where the ruins were situated. She swung Finn's backpack off and rested it on one of the broad fallen stones. He'd given her his kit. Finn never went anywhere without his kit. He'd told her he'd prefer to lose his left arm. What if he needed it?

She walked to the edge of the rocks and stared out over the ocean and lifted her arms over her head, linking her fingers so her shoulders got the benefit of the stretch. What on earth was she going to do now? Stay here? Go back?

No. Going back to the camp would be stupid. It would be better to wait here than trek back through the jungle for an hour and risk getting lost. Finn had said they had a job to do—build a signal fire. Even though she might not be able to light it, she could pile the wood up nice and high, no problem. And then it would all be ready when Finn and the others turned up again.

She didn't let herself think any further about when that might be, even though she feared Finn had been pretty specific. One hour at a time. She was only going to think about the next hour. And she could cope with being alone for sixty minutes, no problem.

It took more than an hour to collect all the wood she'd need, and then almost another hour to stack it the right way. She had to tear it down the first time, realising too late that she'd worked on autopilot, hadn't thought things through. A signal fire would need to catch quickly and burn brightly. It would also need to produce smoke—and lots of it. And that wasn't the kind of fire she'd built. She'd reproduced what they'd done in their camp every evening, where longevity was important and smoke undesirable.

When she finished the second fire she was really thirsty. She took a couple of sips of water from her canteen and then screwed the lid back on. Best to conserve that. There were some coconut trees nearby, so maybe she could gather some of the fallen fruit. Young ones would be nicer and contain more water, but the effort of climbing up to get them would probably burn up more calories than they'd provide, and she needed to conserve her energy.

Either way, she was going to need a knife to get them open. She just hoped that the smaller one Finn always kept in his backpack was up to the job.

The pack was still sitting on the stone she'd plonked it on when she'd first arrived, and she walked over to it, unzipped the main compartment and pulled the edges back to have a good look inside.

Instantly her focus was drawn to a long shape, half-hidden by a balled up shirt. She reached into the bag and drew it out slowly.

Finn's machete. Not strapped to his lower leg, but here, still in its sheath.

Why?

She felt the weight of it in her open palms and stared at it as it lay there. She took a step back and stared at it some more, a frown creasing her features. There was only one sensible reason she could think of why Finn would have *deliberately* left his machete behind.

He really *wasn't* coming back until morning.

'What's she doing?' Simon leaned over the boxy black monitor and squinted. 'She's just standing there. Do you think she's going to cry?'

A ripple of discomfort passed through the tent that had now become *Fearless Finn's* mobile production suite. Barry and Tim shifted uncomfortably. None of them liked female tears. Made them feel helpless, even when they were on a tiny ten-inch screen and the female in question was a quarter of a mile away. Give them snakes and spiders any day.

'No,' Finn said quietly, moving closer, and glancing at one of the other four monitors to get an alternative view of his celebrity guest star.

Simon puffed out a breath and ran a hand through his hair.

'I hope you're right. We had enough waterworks last week from Toby when he realised he was doing his final night solo.' He checked his watch quickly. 'Mind you, it did take him until almost midnight... Action star, my foot.'

Finn tuned Simon out. He'd heard this particular rant before and he was most interested in the slender figure being filmed by several hidden cameras placed strategically round the ruins. When she put the machete down on the rock and put her hands on her hips, Finn wanted to smile, but the warm churning in his stomach made it difficult.

You can do this, he urged her silently. *This is your chance. Your fate tonight is in your hands. You can panic and freak out like the previous guest star or you can choose to use everything I've taught you in the last seven days. Your choice whether you survive or fail.*

He watched closely to see what she'd do next, hoping his gut feeling wasn't going to let him down for once. Allegra had done well this week. Really well. But while she'd been excellent at following his lead, her success rate when she'd been left to her own devices had been a little patchier.

After a few moments her hands dropped from her hips. She marched over to the signal fire she'd built near the edge of the ruins and started pulling it apart, flinging palm branches and bits of wood behind her.

'No!'

His outburst echoed round the tent, which was pretty clever, seeing as the old canvas structure wasn't supposed to facilitate such a sound. Everyone else stopped what they were doing and stared at him. Just as well that Dave was still out filming Allegra from a distance, because he really would have given Finn some stick.

He feigned shock at their reaction. 'What? It was a nicely constructed fire, that's all.'

He turned back to the monitor to hide the heat creeping up his neck. It must have migrated there from his stomach, which was now feeling jittery and cold. He'd expected more of her than this. More than a temper tantrum. Perhaps he'd just been blinded by the tropical sun this week and she really was a prima donna after all.

Monitor four showed her from a different view, and he switched to that one now. What *was* she doing? She seemed to be sorting through the wood, tossing it into smaller piles closer to the lone remaining wall...

Suddenly Finn laughed out loud.

He knew *exactly* what she was doing!

She'd worked out that if she was staying the night there she'd need a different type of fire—one that would burn slowly for hours, not blaze then die out after twenty minutes.

He was so proud of her he wanted to run the quarter mile through the jungle to the ruins and kiss her again.

That would be impossible, of course. So he cemented his attention on the monitors, stacked on a folding camping table at one end of their large working/living/sleeping space.

Allegra had built a new fire now, in the centre of the ruins. Camera two zoomed in on her as she gathered the knife and flint he'd left in his backpack for her and then crouched down, using a fallen stone as a base for her tinder.

Another monitor, another angle. Even closer, this one. Lines appeared on her forehead as she concentrated, and Finn found his own brow wrinkling in sympathy. Again and again she struck the flint. Sparks flew occasionally, but they were never enough. He could see what she was doing wrong. Sometimes she waited too long before she blew on the dried grass, sometimes it was too much too soon.

Slow down. Let your instincts guide you.

He knew she could do it if she didn't give up.

And Allegra refused to give up, until she had to stop, stand up and stretch out her aching shoulder muscles. He could see the frustration radiating from her, even in the shot where her back was to the camera. It was there in her stance, the clenched knuckles at her side.

Relax.

Once she'd stretched, she crouched down and kept going. Finn wanted to cheer. Even Simon stopped scribbling notes and watched.

'Still disappointed poor old Anya Pirelli had to pull out?' he asked, giving Finn a sly look over his shoulder.

Finn kept his face still and his tone deadpan. 'Absolutely gutted.'

Simon chuckled as he turned round and picked up his pen again. 'Thought so.'

Dave appeared through the tent flap some time later, camera in hand. 'Need a new battery,' he said and dumped it on one of the folding camping tables that were holding the production equipment. 'Got some great shots of her working her way through the jungle, but she almost spotted me following her once or twice.'

Finn mumbled a response. He wasn't sure what he actually said. He was too busy watching Allegra at her second attempt at fire starting. She'd broken off a couple of hours ago to make a shelter—a lean-to, using the stone wall as one side. She hadn't built a platform, but she'd remembered she could at least raise the bamboo floor a few inches by using more poles for support. Not bad, Finn thought. She'd used her head and hadn't just tried to replicate the shelter they'd had on the other beach.

Once she'd finished that, she'd turned her attention back to the fire. With no more success than the first attempt, unfortunately.

Finn glanced out of the tent opening at the darkening sky. Another fifteen minutes and she'd really need the warmth and protection a fire would give her. Without it, she'd have a really miserable last night on the island. He didn't want her last memory of it to cloud all the other wonderful things she'd experienced.

Something blunt but insistent poked him in the ribs. It still wasn't enough to make him tear his gaze from the bank of monitors—especially as he suspected the source of pain was one of Dave's pudgy fingers.

'See?' Barry said from the other end of the tent, where he was stretched out on a sleeping mat. 'I told you. He hasn't changed position for the last forty minutes.'

Had it really been that long?

He had one hand on the table and was leaning forward, feet planted one behind the other. A quick inventory of his muscles and joints revealed that he was indeed rather stiff. He straightened, keeping his eyes on monitor three, and did a few shoulder rolls.

'Lo, he moves,' Dave said dryly. 'It's a miracle.'

Finn snorted. 'Don't know why you're making such a fuss. We all crowded round to watch Toby when he did his final challenge, didn't we?'

'Yes, but that's because it was so darn funny watching him cry and ask for his mummy.' There was a creaking noise behind him as Dave dropped into one of the canvas folding chairs. 'She's all right, this one.'

Barry piped up, fancying himself as Dave's sidekick. 'You can stand down, Finn. She's doing okay.' He pulled himself up and came to stand beside Finn, and Finn didn't care for the slimy edge to his voice when he grinned and said, '*More* than okay, that girl.'

Finn's reply as unrepeatable.

And Allegra wasn't okay. She still had no fire.

He leaned forward again, placing his palm on the table and ignoring the creak of his protesting muscles, and turned his attention back to the monitor.

After twenty minutes solid of trying to get a fire going— at one point getting enough sparks to light the tinder, but not managing to get the kindling to light—Allegra suddenly threw down the knife, straightened her legs and looked sky-ward.

She stood still. So still Finn wasn't entirely sure she was breathing, and then she buried her face in her hands. The low howl of frustration, picked up by a hidden microphone and transmitted to speakers either side of the main monitor, made Finn feel like a caged tiger.

She needed him.

He couldn't stand here and watch her like that. He had to go to her.

The urge intensified when she pulled her face from her hands. Simon, who was operating the remote-controlled cam-eras, zoomed in closer, and now Finn could see how the set-ting sun had picked out a single vertical track down each cheek, making them sparkle. He almost pressed a finger to the monitor screen, but reined himself in just in time. No point in giving the terrible two back there even more ammunition.

Allegra's face disappeared from shot and he started. Camera three had been in too close to follow her when she'd suddenly moved, and Finn frantically searched the other mon-itors for a sign of her.

His heart rate slowed. She hadn't fallen or run or panicked. She'd merely crouched again and had picked up the knife and flint.

He let out the breath he'd been holding. So brave. So deter-mined. This time he left a smudgy fingerprint on the monitor and he didn't care who saw it.

Okay. He'd had enough of this.

He marched over to the pile of kit he'd left on his sleeping mat and started strapping his spare knife to his calf. Then he pulled his trouser leg back down.

Simon turned round. 'What are you up to?'

Finn just kept getting ready. It was perfectly obvious what he was doing. He was getting ready to rescue Allegra.

'Finn?'

He pulled a long-sleeved shirt from the pile and put it on over his T-shirt and turned to face his producer. 'I'm going. You can't stop me. We just can't leave her like that!'

Simon stood up. 'That's not the deal with the celeb guests and you know it.'

'Tell that to someone who cares.'

And then he strode from the tent into the twilight. He had mere minutes before complete darkness fell now.

'Finn!'

He ignored Simon's angry yell.

He had to go to her. He couldn't abandon her when she needed him. He couldn't stand by and do nothing. So he was breaking a rule or two. He did it all the time. And he'd never heard Simon complain before—especially if he got a good shot out of it.

'Finn!'

He paused, right on the verge of stepping from the clearing they'd chosen for their camp and into the jungle. There had been a different tone to Simon's voice. Less angry. More urgent.

He ran back towards the tent, his heart pounding with fear now, not frustration. 'What?'

Simon appeared through the tent flap, grinning. 'She did it!'

Finn pushed past him and rushed to the bank of monitors. Sure enough, there in the centre of each one, bathed in warm orange glow was Allegra. Through the speakers he could hear her laughing quietly to herself.

His hands dropped to his sides and his face fell as Simon slapped him on the back.

'The girl done good,' he said, before going back to his camera controls and adjusting a shot.

Finn knew he should be laughing, too. Smiling, at least. But he'd been all revved up to go, to see her, and now there was no need. What was he supposed to do with all this adren-

alin crashing round his system now? If he couldn't take flight
and go to Allegra, the only other option was *fight,* and he was
pretty sure Simon wouldn't want him punching anyone.

He looked at the tent door, flapping in the cool evening
breeze.

He could still go.

One more night with Allegra on the island. One more night
of feeling as if they were parts of a two-piece puzzle, where
he could wrap himself around her and hold her to him. Keep
her there.

So she didn't need him. Who cared? He could still go…

Why?

The question slid into his brain so innocently that he hardly
noticed it at first.

Isn't it because *you* need *her?*

No.

It wasn't that. He just needed to… He just needed…
Allegra.

Finn couldn't find a word to replace her name, no matter how hard he tried. That was bad, wasn't it? Really bad.
Because it showed just how far things had gone. It showed
just how badly he'd gone off course without even realising.

Finn McLeod was Mr Self-Sufficiency. The TV adverts
for the show said so. He didn't need anything but a good pair
of hiking boots, his knife and a flint. That was all. No extra-
neous baggage weighing him down.

For that reason he turned away from the tent door and
parked himself in the chair next to his cameraman. Dave
chuckled and handed him a bottle of water. Finn would much
rather have had a cold beer. The perfect beverage for swap-
ping adventure stories and embellishing near-death experiences with the other blokes, because that was what he made
sure they did for the next few hours. And Finn made equally
sure that he didn't glance at the bank of monitors once.

* * *

Allegra woke face down in a pile of palm leaves and peeled her face from her forearm. Even before she focused on the fuzzy orange glow outside the shelter she realised her fire had lasted. She could feel the warmth on her face. She blinked. It wasn't big, but it was still flickering away.

She'd done it.

A surge of triumph pushed the sleep further back in her consciousness and she sat up and yawned.

The sky was still dark overhead, but near the horizon it was turning pale. Morning was mere minutes away.

Back home, a view of the moment night turned to day was always blocked by the skyline; but here there were no Georgian townhouses or glass and steel creations to hide it from her. And, since this new beach faced eastwards, she was going to have a completely uninterrupted view of the sunrise, maybe her first ever.

She hauled herself out of the shelter, determined to make the most of it, and tossed another couple of logs on the fire, hoping they'd keep it going until she worked out what she was going to eat for breakfast. Her mouth was dry, so she rooted around in her shelter for her canteen and drank deeply.

They'd be here soon. Finn had said so. She supposed she should have been disappointed she hadn't been able to spend her last night on the island with Finn, but the sense of achievement wouldn't allow her to mope. And she'd felt connected to him all night—every time she'd used a skill he'd taught her.

The morning was so perfect she almost wanted to cry.

And not just because of the scenery. She'd be seeing Finn soon. Her ears began to tingle at the very thought of it. Just the thought of laying eyes on that floppy dark hair, those laughing eyes, made her jump to her feet and run to the edge of the fort. Where she was going and what she was looking for she wasn't sure; she just needed to move.

Oh, today was going to be glorious. Because today she felt as if she could do anything. Even the impossible.

Especially the impossible.

Because today she was going to stop being such a coward and let Finn McLeod know exactly how much she needed him in her life.

A slap on the back from a large, overenthusiastic hand brought Finn to consciousness. He didn't open his eyes straight away—they seemed to be welded shut. And what was he sleeping up against? A rock?

He prised his eyelids open and blinked. The blurry information his brain was receiving was just about enough for him to work out that, somehow, during the course of the night his chair had worked itself from the other side of the tent to just in front of the monitor rack, and the cold hard surface supporting his cheek was in fact one of the folding tables.

'It's time to go,' Simon said softly, and Finn realised the whole crew had gathered round him. Or, rather, he was in the way of their attempt to watch the monitors. He sat up just fast enough to make little silver flecks dance at the edge of his vision.

Only inches from his face, multiplied four times, was a slender figure at the edge of the ruins, looking towards the horizon.

He swallowed, his throat dry and thick, and his slumbering pulse began to wake.

The first glint of bright, warm light burst above the horizon, as if it could hardly wait to get the day started. Allegra held her breath. For some reason the sight made her unbearably excited. She began to move, clambering down the rocks at the edge of the ruins. Once her feet hit sand she ran down the beach towards the shore. It seemed to be the proper thing to do, to greet the rising sun. And there was no one else here to do it.

As a soft golden stripe appeared on the horizon she started to grin.

She'd done it, hadn't she? She'd really done it! Survived a whole night on her own in the wilderness. Finn had been right—she felt wonderful.

She'd built her own shelter, found her own food and made a fire. Not skills she'd need back home, but that hardly seemed to matter. At the moment she felt that if she could do all this, there were no limits to what she could accomplish back on familiar turf. She could certainly go back home and face whatever music was coming her way, make some decisions about what to do next.

What she couldn't do was just stand there. She needed to *do* something, let this glowing feeling she had inside her out somehow.

So she ran, her bare feet leaving dents in the damp sand— deeper at the heel, shallower at the toes. And when half the untouched shoreline of the smallish beach had been branded as hers she decided to do a cartwheel. Just because she could. Just to change the pattern of marks in the sand, to see fingers instead of toes, two starfish handprints amongst her running tracks.

That done, she started making other shapes in the sand by turning, jumping, drawing arcs with her toes as her hands and fingers drew them in the air.

And then the oddest thing happened—it started to rain. She glanced up to see the clouds up ahead, blown over the island from the west, but off in the east the sun still hovered unobscured, painting the bottom of the sky with peaches and pinks and yellows.

She paused for a moment, looking back at her tracks across the beach. It was almost shocking to see the physical evidence of her movement, as ice skaters did with their traces and figures, but there it all was—her dance of joy, carved in the sand for all to see.

But she didn't stop yet. Couldn't. Even though the tiny drops of water peppering her skin were picking up their tempo.

It was all still bubbling inside of her, wanting to be let out. So she did. She spun around fast, her arms flung wide, laughing, and almost toppled over face first into the sand. When gravity forced her to change direction to save herself she used that momentum into a leap, and then another.

She'd swear that this morning she could finally fulfil the illusion ballet promised: that she'd finally fly.

Simon's voice crackled over the walkie-talkie. 'I still can't see her.'

Finn, Dave, Barry and Tim were standing in the centre of the ruins, staring at Allegra's shelter. The rain was splashing into the fire, causing the hot logs to sizzle. Close up, Finn could see the lean-to wouldn't have lasted more than a few nights without improvement, but that hardly mattered. It had done the job last night, and that was what counted.

He turned in a circle, his hand shielding his eyes from the rising sun. Simon had radioed through about five minutes ago, while they'd been between the two camps, to say he'd lost sight of Allegra on the monitors. She couldn't have gone far, surely? The rain would bring her back to the shelter pretty soon.

While Dave and Barry got some shots of Allegra's temporary home, Finn strode to the edge of the ruins, his eyes restlessly scanning from left to right and back again. That was when he spotted the footprints heading off down the beach.

Moments later he was standing on the sand, frozen by the beauty of the scene in front of him—and he hadn't even noticed the sunrise yet.

She was dancing.

Not the pretty, precise movements he'd seen her do on stage. This was sometimes graceful, sometimes clumsy. Her clothes were dotted with large rain spots and her hair had fallen out of her ponytail and was starting to look damp and stringy, but what she was doing eclipsed all of that. It was wild and free and definitely, definitely beautiful. Even when she stumbled and landed on her rear end. Because this dance wasn't just movement, it was truth. This dance *was* Allegra.

And, right at that moment, Finn realised he'd reached the end point of the journey he'd started with her a week ago. He had a sense of things falling into place, that something permanent and inevitable had just happened.

He was finally there. His ultimate destination.

And now it made sense why he'd never been able to find it, why he'd always had to search one more place, try one more map reference. Like most great discoveries, this one had a twist to it, something Finn hadn't expected or planned for.

Not for one second had Finn McLeod thought that his ultimate destination, the end to all his restlessness, might not be a place but a person. That elusive beauty wasn't to be found in the great outdoors, but in this woman. All of that in one tiny frame. It must have been a powerful miracle that had put it there.

Allegra paused in her dance and spotted him just as the full terror of his situation hit him.

He had to move on.

Because Finn McLeod always moved on. But he didn't run away; that was cowardly. He was always moving *towards* the next destination, not *away* from where he'd just been, so he needed a plausible sounding reason to pin his departure on.

She started to run towards him—not pretty little gallops, but full-out sprinting—and Finn had to dig his heels into the sand to keep himself there. As she came closer he saw that a grin was lighting up her face. She did a cartwheel just before she reached him, clean and precise and elegant, and landed in a little jump in front of him.

'I did it, Finn! I did it!'

He wanted to smile, but the need to clench his jaw to stop his teeth from chattering prevented it. 'Yes, you did.'

But he discovered he didn't need to smile back. His gaze moved upwards from her lips and teeth to her eyes. There it was again. That feeling of something finishing, of something being knotted and tied…

'Oh…you were right, Finn! There's nothing like this. I feel so alive!' Her smile outgrew her words, stopping her from talking for a few seconds, while she shook her head in disbelief. 'Thank you. Thank you for giving this to me…'

She stepped forward and touched her damp and slightly sandy fingertips to his cheekbones. Finn stopped breathing.

And then she kissed him, a sweet, slow touching of the lips, full of gratitude and so much more. It was the briefest of moments, and she did it again, just because once wasn't enough.

Once wasn't nearly enough.

But he peeled her fingertips from his face, pulled his lips from hers.

'Allegra…'

She rested her forehead against his shoulder. He could hear the rain slapping on her scalp and his, see it running through her hair and down her face. She closed her eyes.

So beautiful…

An idea formed in his head. A reason. A very good reason. One he could just about buy into himself. One that would make leaving the right thing instead of the wrong thing.

He knew now that one could be selfish with beauty. Hadn't he had the urge last night to rush in and rob her of her chance to discover she could do it on her own? If he'd followed his instincts, she wouldn't be feeling this now, wouldn't be looking at him as if she were a firework waiting to shoot straight into the sky.

He'd almost put his need above hers. Even worse, he couldn't promise himself he wouldn't do it again. How could he stop himself wanting to limit her, by tying her to him? It was so wrong. Not what *she* needed.

She'd had too much of that in her life already. She needed a chance to stretch her wings and fly, to see if she could do it on her own. He couldn't take that away from her.

Even so, he was weak. Before he told her so, he kissed her, and it was long and sweet and drugging. And it said far more than he'd wanted to say. It gave far too much away.

She smiled against his lips and then tipped her head up to look at him.

No, don't, he wanted to say. Don't look at me like that, like you'd throw all that freedom you've just earned for yourself away on me, because I really don't deserve it. I'm not even man enough to *want* it.

Their fingers were still intertwined and he brought them down so they were between their bodies, the flimsiest of barriers. He wasn't sure if he was holding her fingers to stop her doing anything more, or to prevent himself.

He got his answer when he pulled away and stepped back, letting her hands drop. 'I can't do this for you,' he said hoarsely. 'I can't be this for you.'

She opened her eyes and Finn wished she'd kept them closed. No one should have to witness such bleakness in the eyes of another. He didn't want the guilt of having caused it, but he had no other choice. Allegra's roots had already started to burrow deep inside him. He couldn't let them continue to grow. It wouldn't be good for either of them, and it was better to cut them off now before they got so embedded he wouldn't survive when they were pulled out.

She stood very still, her eyes saying the words before they left her mouth. 'I think I love you.'

The honesty and bravery of her statement slammed into him, making him take yet another step back.

'You told me to make a choice,' she said. 'And I choose you.'

He shook his head. 'That's impossible.'

One corner of her mouth curled in a heartbreaking attempt at a smile. 'I thought I was supposed to "expect the impossible" with you around. Don't you live up to your hype?'

Not even close, he'd discovered. And it was time for her to know that about him.

She kept talking. Finn closed his eyes. He wanted her to stop.

'I feel *I* could do the impossible now, thanks to you,' she added softly.

A spark lit inside him. That was his *out*. In survival situations you always had to have an *out*. He looked away, back at the ruins, as he noticed Tim and Dave watching them from the top of the rocks. Dave had his camera on his shoulder.

'You don't love me,' he said. 'You can't. It's too much, too soon...'

The smile disappeared. The eyes grew huge.

Finn kept going. 'You ran away from your life because you were looking for an escape, and you found me. I can't let you anchor yourself to me instead. It wouldn't be right.'

She shook her head. Stubborn as well as beautiful. Yes, he remembered that now.

'I can't be your escape route, Allegra. I can't rescue you.'

It sounded so reasonable, so sane. Then why did he feel one step down from a leech on the evolutionary scale?

'But I know you feel the same way. I—'

'I can't,' he said firmly. 'You've been wonderful company this week, but that's all it will ever be. It's not a fairy tale where I can fall instantly in love with someone else, swap partners and then ride off into the sun—' he blinked at the heavy globe on the horizon '—rise.'

He saw it. The moment the poison worked, when it reached her eyes.

'Real life is harder,' he said, feeling steadier now, feeling slightly justified, even. 'You do what you must to survive.'

As he was, right now.

'I'm sorry,' he said. And he really meant it, but his words sounded superficial and hollow.

She looked at him, sadness and anger and longing warring for supremacy on her rain-soaked features.

He didn't have anything left to say, so he turned and walked back up the beach to join his crew—his team—and left her to watch the rain pooling in his footsteps, making little puddles.

CHAPTER ELEVEN

PUDDLES. They were so very *London,* Allegra decided, as her plane taxied towards the gate at Heathrow. Outside the dirty plane window the sky was grey. The terminal building was grey. The tarmac was grey, and even the flat puddles collecting on it were grey.

Welcome home, Allegra.

Home to what, she wasn't sure. She was half tempted to stay in the terminal building and run away again, book a flight to somewhere pretty and forget about everything. Everyone. Especially *someone.*

They'd shared a speedboat off the island and the same hotel for one night before going their separate ways. They hadn't discussed what had happened on the beach, or the night of the thunderstorm. In fact, they'd hardly even talked. There had been post-island interviews to complete, and she'd had the feeling Finn was deliberately keeping out of her way. Then she'd flown east—back home to London—and he'd headed west. He hadn't told her exactly where.

Didn't matter, though. She still felt as if a part of herself had gone with him.

It wasn't fair. She would have been able to let him go easily if she'd really believed that was what he wanted, but she'd seen his eyes when he'd given her the brush-off. So different from the way he'd looked at her when he'd kissed her. But *exactly* the same as the shuttered expression he'd worn the previous morning when he'd been hiding something, keeping her secret challenge from her.

At first that 'no entry' look had given her hope, because she'd known it was a lie. Now it just made her angry.

The plane trundled to a halt and passengers began grabbing their things from overhead lockers. Allegra stayed in her seat and let them scurry about. She wasn't in a hurry, after all. What did she have to come back to? Her father would be furious with her—as he had every right to be—and her career was in tatters.

Thankfully, she didn't have anything but hand luggage, so at least the process of getting through the airport was quicker than it could have been. As she exited Immigration, she spotted a burly form she recognised.

'Dave?'

He turned and smiled at her, which left her speechless. She didn't think she'd seen his lips and teeth do that before. But they really didn't have that much to say to each other, so after the awkward greeting they both just stood there.

'Thank you,' she said.

'Sorry,' he said at the same time.

She frowned. 'What for? It was my choice to do the show, and I enjoyed it most of the time.'

'I'm talking about the Fearless One,' he said, his face reverting to his much more familiar and strangely comforting scowl. 'If it makes you feel any better, I've always said the bloke was an A-grade idiot.'

Allegra sighed. It hadn't been the camera that had had the all-seeing eye, had it? It had been Dave. And, apparently, he really had seen everything.

'Thanks,' she said for the second time, even though it hadn't made her feel better at all.

Dave nodded and wandered off towards Customs.

Allegra stood there, too angry with Finn to move. She

wanted to shake him, make him understand what he was turning his back on, but she couldn't, could she? Because Finn
wasn't here. He was probably thousands of miles away. She
shook her head instead, still not quite ready to face the fact
that while she might have chosen him, Finn clearly hadn't
chosen her back.

As she neared the Arrivals gate she could hear a lot of
noise. There must be a lot of people out there. Perhaps somebody famous was about to arrive?

Flashguns fired in rapid succession as she turned the corner into the arrivals hall. She glanced round. The elderly couple with the trolley she'd been walking behind just looked like
regular holidaymakers back from a bit of winter sun. Clearly,
she should have recognised them.

Still the flashguns fired at a dizzying speed. Allegra held
her hand up in front of her face, palm out, to deflect the ret-
ina-searing pops of light. The sooner she was out of this, the
better. All she wanted to do was slink away home and lick
her wounds, leave the elderly couple to their moment of glory.
Maybe they were lottery winners or something.

But then the general roar of journalists' shouts crystallised
into actual words.

'Allegra!'

'Miss Martin? Over here!'

That was her name. These people were here for *her*? What
on earth had she done to warrant this?

A woman, not much older than herself, lunged over the
barrier and thrust a Dictaphone her way. 'Allegra! Why exactly did you drop out of *The Little Mermaid* and run away?'

She shook her head and moved on. Really? All this fuss
for her? It was hardly the golden age of ballet anymore, when
ballerinas had been treated like movie queens. Why would
anyone care if she missed a performance or two? They certainly didn't seem very impressed when she *had* shown up,

and there were plenty of other dancers rehearsed and ready to step into her shoes.

She moved more quickly now, glad she only had the one bag hoisted over her shoulder and wasn't slowed down by a trolley. Mind you, she could have used it as a battering ram, so maybe it would have been a good idea. She dipped her head and ignored them all, leaving the catcalls and outrageous questions unheeded.

'Allegra! Can you confirm reports you've been in an exclusive clinic after a breakdown and the desert island story is a cover-up?'

She was tempted to laugh, but she put her ballet face on and kept her features neutral. Where did people come up with these ideas? They must try to outdo each other in some kind of twisted contest. The best thing to do was not to react. Just keep walking and she'd soon be out of there.

But right near the end of the barriers, a whole scrum of reporters waited, making a wall that had closed around the elderly couple and had blocked off her exit. She slowed her pace significantly and started looking around for a gap—any gap, no matter how small. How was she going to get round them? And what were they going to do? Follow her home on the Tube?

She was starting to panic a little when she spotted a tall, solid mass in the crowd, grim and unsmiling. *Dave.* She'd never been so pleased to see that grumpy mug in all of her life. He was looking straight at her, and his eyes were speaking volumes. *Stick with me,* they said, *and I'll get you out of here in one piece.*

She breathed out and picked up speed. As she reached him he put a protective tree trunk of an arm around her shoulders and steered her through the crowd. One bright spark couldn't resist a parting shot, though.

'Miss Martin! Rumour has it you ran away for a steamy

week in paradise with your secret lover, Finn McLeod. Care to comment?'

The gaggle of journalists hushed, eager to catch her answer.

'How do you think his fiancée's going to feel about that?' the reporter added.

Allegra didn't say anything, of course. But she'd swivelled her head to look at the man before she could tell herself not to. Her mouth was slightly open and her eyes full of guilt and panic. Not quite the truth, what he'd said, but close enough to hit a nerve. She didn't need to say a word; her face had said far too much already.

The picture—and headline—in tomorrow morning's paper was going to be a doozie.

Allegra stood in her basement kitchen opposite her father, her overnight bag at her feet. Neither of them had said anything in the last sixty seconds.

Dave had whisked her out of the airport and into a car the producers of *Fearless Finn* had provided when they'd realised what kind of reception had been waiting for Allegra at the airport. Anything to keep their guest star happy—especially as her show might just get them the highest ratings they'd ever had. However, the journey had been much quicker than her planned slog on the Tube and, as a result, she'd had hardly any time to get her head ready for this moment.

'It was a bit crazy at the airport,' she said finally.

Great opening line, Allegra. Really eloquent.

Her father nodded to a tabloid paper that lay, unfolded, on the kitchen table. 'I'm not surprised.'

She took a couple of steps forward, then stopped. That was *her* on the front! A horrible picture of her, looking all tired and tortured. When on earth had that been taken?

'*Runaway ballerina thought to be on tropical island hideaway*', the headline screamed. There was even a small box down on one side with a picture of Finn and his fiancée. They'd managed to find a photo of him that made him look really...shady...at first glance. Closer inspection led her to believe he'd been about to say something to the photographer—something funny, knowing Finn—but the shutter had closed when his eyelids were half-shut and his mouth halfway between smile and joke, and he'd ended up looking both sly and arrogant.

She flicked the first page over. *More* photos! More words—all about her and Finn!

'The press got wind of your...disappearance...and couldn't resist making a meal of it,' her father said dryly. 'I take it there's no truth in these rumours that you're having an affair with a married man?'

Allegra's mouth dropped open and she shook her head. 'N...no! And he's not married. He *was* engaged, but...' Oh, it was so complicated, and what was the use? She hung her head. 'I only met the man last week and, no, there's nothing between us.'

Nothing at all.

Her father exhaled and ran a hand through his hair, then he pulled out one of the kitchen chairs and sat down at the table. 'Then why?' he asked, looking fragile and crushed—the way he'd been after her mother had died. 'Wasn't your life good enough for you? What more could I have done?'

Allegra was momentarily speechless. She hadn't expected this at all. Lectures and scoldings, yes, but not this broken man sitting at his kitchen table, looking confused and sad. She'd had no idea she had the power to reduce him to this, and the realisation brought no joy, only guilt and regret.

She went and stood behind his chair, bent over and pressed her cheek against his. Then she folded her arms around him as tears slid down her cheeks. 'I'm sorry,' she whispered. 'I didn't mean to hurt you—I didn't mean to hurt anyone—I just...'

She kissed his temple softly, then just held him. More tears fell as she realised he was shaking just as much as she was.

'Please, Daddy, don't…'

She hugged him tighter and his hand came up and gently rested on her forearm. They stayed like that, breathing, for a few moments and then she skirted round the table to sit opposite him, maintaining contact as long as she could, leaving her hand on his shoulder, and then she drew his hands into hers across the table.

When had her father become so old?

When had *she?*

Because something had changed between them. She was still his daughter, but she knew, deep down, that she wasn't his little girl any more.

'Thank you,' she said, 'for being my protector and champion, for looking after me when I needed you to, but—'

His eyes seemed to get greyer. 'But you don't need me any more.'

She shook her head softly. 'No, that's not what I meant. I just…'

How did she put this?

'I needed you to do those things for me when I was growing up, but I've finished now. I finished a long time ago. And I'm perfectly capable of making my own decisions—' she glanced at the open paper on the table '—and my own mistakes.' A dark flash of humour passed between them. 'But I still need you, Dad. Just not in the same way…'

Her father nodded. 'I understand,' he said. 'And I'm sorry, too. I should have let you have your wings before now, but it was so hard…' He looked away. 'Your mother…she left before I was ready to let her go.'

And you held onto me instead.

Her throat thickened, and she squeezed his hand. He didn't need to say the rest.

Her gaze wandered to the paper again. 'The company?

The Artistic Director…?' She scrunched her face up as she looked back at her father. 'Just how bad is it?'

He gave her a weary smile. 'I won't say that tops weren't blown at the Opera House directly after you left, but you've actually been quite lucky.'

She stared back at him. 'They're not going to fire me?'

He shook his head. 'All this…furore…has sent ticket sales through the roof for *The Little Mermaid.* You might get a few stony silences and disapproving looks when you go back, but in these hard economic times they can't argue with the box office. And since you're the ballerina the press can't stop talking about at the moment, they want you back.'

Allegra wasn't sure how she felt about that. When she'd thought her career was on the skids it had been scary, but it had been kind of liberating, too. She wasn't sure she wanted to get back on that treadmill again.

'You're saying they might consider offering me another lead role in the future?'

'I'm saying they want you to do Saturday's performance.'

Allegra's eyes bulged. 'What?'

Her father ran a hand over his face and sighed. 'You have no idea of the media storm you created when you ran away, do you?'

Her eyebrows arched high. 'It must have been a really slow news week.'

That made him laugh. She liked that. She hardly ever made her father laugh.

'I don't suppose that hurt,' he said. 'But the "runaway ballerina" story seems to have caught the nation's interest. The press have been in a frenzy trying to work out why you'd gone and where you were. There's been constant speculation about when you'd come back and if you'd dance again.'

Allegra made a scoffing noise. 'Even though they all seem to think I've lost my magic?'

'Even then. The role's yours, if you want it.'

Allegra slumped back in her chair. That just didn't make sense. She'd been a bad, bad ballerina. No truly dedicated dancer would abandon a production after the opening night and leave the company in the lurch that way. It wasn't the way her world worked, no matter what the papers said.

But with the funding cuts and tough economic times, maybe the rules were changing.

It had been more than a week since she'd done a class— her body would be totally out of shape. She couldn't do this, could she? Just step back into her old life, using her sudden notoriety to grease the way? Did she even want to?

She made eye contact with her father. 'You said *when* I go back.'

He nodded. 'I did.'

She licked her lips then spoke slowly. 'I'm saying, *if* I go back…'

His jaw slackened slightly. 'Allegra…'

'I know, Daddy. I know.' She pushed her chair away from the table. 'But before I make that decision I really think I need a good night's sleep.'

For a moment she thought he was going to argue with her, but then he stood also and came round the table to kiss her on the cheek. 'Then sleep well,' was all he said.

The coffee shop on the corner of her street wasn't usually a final destination for Allegra but merely a pitstop on her way to the company's rehearsal studios or the theatre. This morning, however, she sat with her coffee in a ceramic mug at a tiny round table in the window, watching the rest of Notting Hill bustle by.

She had a meeting with the Artistic Director at three. Her fate would be decided then. Not by him, but by herself. She held all the power today. It was a novel feeling for Allegra and, had other more attention-grabbing emotions not been clouding her view, she might have relished it.

She sighed and blew on her latte before sinking her lips into the warm foam and taking a sip. The one situation she really wanted to be able to bend to her will was completely out of her grasp, and she would have given anything to trade that power from her career to her personal life; but, unfortunately, the ball was in Finn's court, and not only was he not returning it, she didn't think he was even playing her game.

It was unbearable, this empty feeling. It made her restless. She had to keep moving because it was the only way to ignore the deep, aching pit that had developed inside her. The only way to avoid being sucked down into it piece by piece.

She picked up her coffee cup and marched over to the counter. 'Can I have a paper cup and a lid?' she asked the barista. The girl shrugged and handed them over. Allegra poured her latte into the cup, wedged the lid on top and handed the empty mug back to her. 'Thanks,' she said, and strode out of the coffee shop in the direction of the nearest Tube.

She couldn't wait to see the Artistic Director. She was going to see him now. Maybe being face to face with him would solidify her decision.

However, a trill on her mobile phone halted her just after she'd left Covent Garden station. She pulled it out of her pocket.

An unidentified number. Her heart began to race. Had Finn finally decided to lob a ball her way? He could easily have got her number from Simon.

When she answered, she sounded a little breathless. 'Hello?'

'Allegra Martin?'

Her chest deflated fully in one long puff. No curling Scottish accent. No deep rumble of adventure behind the words.

'Yes,' she said wearily.

'Hi. My name's Danny Gold and I work for the *London*

Post. My paper would like to do an exclusive with you on the Runaway Ballerina story.'

'No, thanks,' she said quickly, but it seemed the man had been ready for that.

'There will, of course, be a fee involved.' He mentioned a figure that made Allegra's eyes pop. 'For you to keep or give to charity, whatever you wish…'

Wishing? That didn't get anyone anywhere, did it? She'd learned that lesson quite nicely, thank you.

'This is your chance, Allegra, to take control of what's being said about you—to put the record straight. And whether you want to mention what happened—or didn't happen—between you and Finn McLeod, well, that's totally up to you.'

The unctuous edge that had crept into his voice on the last sentence told Allegra exactly which way he hoped she'd fall. It made her want to disinfect the ear that was pressed to her phone.

'I—'

'Don't decide yet,' he said in a blatantly phoney non-pressurising manner. 'I'll give you a call back in an hour and give you time to think.' And then he rang off before she had a chance to tell him—in a very un-Allegra-like way—where he could stuff his exclusive.

She snapped her phone closed and started walking again. The nerve of the man! Sell her story, indeed! As if anything she said to him would be reproduced accurately, as if it could help close a trapdoor over the pit and save her from falling in…

She stopped suddenly and a woman with a shopping bag bumped into her from behind, then tutted as she scuttled past.

But it could. A story like that would demand a response. It would *make* Finn face facts. He'd have to do something, wouldn't he? He wouldn't be able to ignore what was simmering between them—or ignore her—if it was splashed all over the front of the newspapers.

No.

That was crazy thinking. Even too outlandish for a mermaid. And it showed just how desperate she was starting to get where Finn was concerned. This wasn't good.

Maybe Finn had been right about her. Maybe this urge to cling to him would poison any possible future relationship. Because cling she would. Like a limpet. At least, that was what she wanted to do.

She stared at the phone. Oh, she could give Danny from the *Post* his 'kiss and tell' if she wanted to, she knew that. She could also run and spin and do a cartwheel right in the middle of Covent Garden piazza. Didn't mean it was a good idea. Didn't mean she might not injure her wrists or crash into someone else and hurt them.

She slid her phone into her coat pocket and carried on along James Street, then turned the corner into the piazza and made her way past the shops under the thick-pillared portico towards the Royal Opera House's main entrance.

Giving this Danny Gold person what he wanted wouldn't change anything.

Okay, it would break the story about Nat and Finn's split, but what good would that do? It really was none of her business, was it? And all the revelation would do was back Finn into a corner, and he'd hate that. Hate her.

She'd spent too much of her life with her back against the wall to want to inflict that on someone else—especially Finn, who needed his freedom.

Finn had made his choice; and she had to let go, give him room to live with it. With one long breath she did it. Released the anger. Released the idea of Finn as hers. It made her feel heavy and breathless and empty, but in a strange way it brought her peace.

When she reached the entrance of the Royal Opera House

she paused for a moment before walking through the revolving door. They all had choices to make and live with, didn't they? And now it was time to make hers.

CHAPTER TWELVE

FINN jumped off the bus in Malcesine and looked around. He'd always wanted to visit the Italian lakes to do some hiking. However, he hadn't expected to come here via Sydney and, granted, he'd have probably preferred July to February, but the mountains were still busy, full of skiers and snowboarders.

He looked up at the mountain to his right, not just dusted with snow but caked with it. The cable car station was only supposed to be five minutes away. If the tourist traffic wasn't too heavy, he might be at the summit of Monte Baldo in under half an hour.

Unfortunately for Finn, it was a glorious day. The sky was clear blue, the sun warm, and the cableway swarming with visitors eager to make the most of the clear conditions to see a snow-draped Lake Garda.

He squeezed himself into one of the rotating cable cars with a host of other people and ended up not being able to see much of the journey, thanks to a couple of outrageous bobble hats. Didn't matter. He'd be at the top soon, and he could find some space away from everyone else, somewhere beautiful where he could finally breathe.

Once at the top, he ignored the crowded café selling hot chocolate by the bucketload and headed straight outside, pulling his gloves on as he did so. He had a map of the area, knew where the ski runs and hiking lodges were, but first he wanted to walk along the flat ridge of the mountain and get the best view of the lake.

He trudged along, head down, ignoring other walkers, and in roughly ten minutes he was standing at the end of the ridge by a rickety-looking wood and wire fence that stopped eager tourists plummeting to their deaths.

The friend who'd told him about this had been right. From here he could see the entire north end of the lake, all the way to Riva del Garda nestling in the shadow of Monte Rochetta, and the view was absolutely stunning.

Finn stood there, waiting for the rush.

It would come soon, he knew it would.

Minutes ticked by and Finn's nose began to get cold. Nothing came. Nothing happened. In fact, he was pretty sure his heart rate had slowed a little.

He turned to face the other direction, where the smooth snowy top of the mountain fell away to reveal the white-topped roofs and church tower of Malcesine, nearly two thousand metres below. A pearly mist hovered above the lake, making it seem as if the town had emerged from a dream.

Still nothing.

Okay, *something*. Just not anything he wanted to feel or think about.

Knowing that if she'd been here he'd have seen her eyes sparkle by now, she'd have turned to look at him and smiled that smile of hers.

Finn rubbed his glove over his face and turned his attention to his boots.

Wow, he was pathetic.

He'd deliberately left her behind, deliberately sought out fresh places that had no connection to her, or even to the TV show—just in case that triggered a memory—and still he couldn't sever whatever it was that joined them.

Suddenly Finn didn't want to hike any more. He wanted to go home. Somewhere warm and familiar. Somewhere he

could just rest his wandering feet and *be*. Sad, really, that he
didn't have one. He had a flat, but it wasn't anything more
than a base, a storage place for all his stuff when he was away.
So where was he supposed to go now?

A cold gust of wind made his cheeks tingle. He set off back
along the ridge to the cable car station and joined the queue
for the ride down. It was just as busy, just as full of people
who thought that because they'd taken a trip to the top and
snapped a few pictures they knew all about mountains now.
If he'd had the energy he would have told them they were
dreaming, kidding themselves. They weren't explorers, no
matter how much they'd spent on their fancy ski jackets. They
were, and always would be, tourists.

Nat's words from a fortnight ago echoed in his head.

That was us, Finn.

He shook his head, even though the car was crowded and
others might see him and think he was losing it.

No. She was wrong. Had to be.

We were tourists.

The car lurched over a pylon and Finn's stomach went with
it.

Allegra had asked him, hadn't she, with those eyes of hers?
She'd asked him to live and breathe and explore with her.
Explore a connection, not to a place or a pretty view, but to
a human being. Even though they were both inexperienced
and the journey was risky. Even though survival wasn't guaranteed.

She'd asked him for more. Not by pushing and demanding but by simply being who she was, showing him there was
more sweetness to be had from life, if only he was brave and
determined enough to climb up and reach for it.

And what had he done? He'd run, telling himself Allegra
had needed her freedom. Bull. It was him who'd needed his.

But it hadn't worked. He hadn't protected himself from
anything.

The hole had still appeared, deep and wide and gaping. The difference was that this time he hadn't been at the mercy of his parents' jobs or army orders. He'd made the decision. It had been his choice.

This was *his* hole. And it didn't feel any better than the other kind.

'*Signor?*'

He turned to find the cable car attendant looking at him. The car was empty, all the other passengers having disembarked, and he was getting impatient looks from the next batch of ticket holders staring at him through the closed glass door on the other side of the car. He mumbled his apologies and exited swiftly.

Then he walked to the nearest café and ordered a hot chocolate. While he waited for it to arrive he rummaged for his mobile phone in his trouser pocket. God bless radio waves and Wi-Fi and mobile phone networks. He had some bookings to sort out and an important call to make.

One that would prove, maybe once and for all, if Finn was really as fearless as his hype said he was.

She stood in the wings, her hair done, costume on, false eyelashes and make-up perfect, trying to hold herself together.

It wasn't easy. Ever since she'd stopped being angry at Finn, a crushing sense of sadness had engulfed her, making her limbs heavy and her movements sluggish. She had no idea how she was going to do anything but drag herself round the stage that night.

She closed her eyes and tried to breathe slowly, gain some sense of calm, because she really wanted this performance to go well. Partly because the world's eyes were on her more than ever, but mostly because this—ballet—was finally her choice.

Not because of who her mother had been. Not because of her father's loss or expectations. Not even because it was the only thing she knew how to do. But because it was a part of her and she really did love it. Rehearsals over the past few days had only confirmed what she'd started to realise on a sunlit beach. How odd that it had taken running away from it to find it again.

The music changed and the corps rushed past her onto the stage. Once again, images flashed through her brain as she waited for her entrance. But this time they weren't second-hand from a TV screen; they were from her own bank of carefully pressed memories.

Finn's smile every time he made a fire. The way he'd reached for her the night of the thunderstorm, such vulnerability in his eyes. All the things those same eyes had told her before he'd backed away and started lying to her.

The violins sang her cue. It was time to go, time to dazzle, even though she felt like letting her legs collapse under her and sobbing into her hands.

She'd thought she'd known all about longing the last time she'd stood here. How presumptuous. How blind. She'd known nothing. Longing had just been an idea, a vague sense of restlessness, but now she knew its taste and its texture. Now longing had a name.

Finn McLeod.

And there was only one way to deal with it, she thought, as she rose onto the balls of her feet and ran onto the empty stage.

She had no voice tonight. She might not even have a soul. But that didn't mean she didn't have anything to say. Just because she wasn't going to sell a story to the papers, it didn't mean she didn't have one. So, as her arm swept over her head and her feet began to move, Allegra began to tell it.

Finn ran up the empty main staircase and glanced at the card rectangle in his hand when he reached the top. *Balcony box 97. Seat 1.* The only destination he cared about at the moment. All the tickets had been sold out, but thank goodness Simon had friends in high places with corporate accounts.

Thank goodness, too, for London cabbies who'd drive at an insane speed from Heathrow, given the right monetary incentive. Too bad, though, that he'd only just made it and wasn't dressed like most of the other theatregoers. He was still wearing his usual practical cargo trousers and shirt and about three layers of plane dirt.

He could hear the muffled orchestra from behind the closed theatre doors, and when he finally burst into his box the house lights were down and there was movement on stage. Finn searched frantically for her and it took only a split second to lock onto her, even though from this height he could hardly see her features and he barely recognised her under the make-up and bright lights. The movement, though, was unmistakable. He knew it was her from the soft grace of her arms, the power and strength in those legs, the emotion radiating out into the audience that squeezed his lungs.

There was a rather impatient cough behind him. He turned round, brows raised.

A thin man in a bow tie was giving him a disapproving look. 'Would you mind sitting down. You're not made of glass, you know.'

Finn dropped into the empty seat, muttering his apologies.

But he didn't want to sit. He wanted to stand, to run, to jump. He wanted to climb down over this darn balcony and rush to the front of the stage. Of course, he would need to be able to see straight for that, and at the moment just the sight of that tall blond guy manhandling Allegra was fogging his vision. He'd better keep his hands in the right places or Finn would be tempted to use his machete. Or he would have done if he'd remembered to strap it to his leg.

Hands off! he wanted to shout. *Mine!*

But the knowledge that he'd blown that chance kept him silent and in his seat. However, his irritation melted away as the ballet continued. He hardly saw her partner any more because all he could watch was Allegra. He'd known she was good, but this...

She was blowing him away.

And from the hushed electricity of the auditorium, he guessed he wasn't alone. No whispers, no creaking seats. Hardly even a movement. Over two thousand people seemed to be holding their breath in concert.

It wasn't just the grace and elegance of her movements; it was the way she lived and breathed the character. A pure spirit far too good for the blind prince who couldn't see the beauty right under his nose. And when the dunce walked away, believing his fulfilment lay elsewhere, Finn wanted to punch the guy.

How dare you break that brave heart? he wanted to shout. *Look what you did! You crushed it with your dirty boots, and even then you still couldn't destroy it. There it is, living and breathing and dancing in front of you, and you still haven't the courage to see it. Not until it's far too late.*

Please let it not be too late.

The final curtain fell and Finn slumped in his seat, as exhausted as if he'd done a ten mile run with a rucksack full of rocks. And when the curtain rose again and it was Allegra's turn to step forward the entire audience rose to their feet. The whistles and cheers seemed to go on for hours. Finn, still dazed, managed to stand and join them. He'd had plenty of practice shouting out his joy, after all.

But the applause eventually did start to die away. People began to sit down. Finn looked nervously at the edges of the red velvet curtain, fearing a twitch that would signal they were going to close, that they'd hide her from him and he might never get the chance to tell her what he needed to say.

He'd never get to her if he tried to go backstage, would he? The whole place would be swarming. It was now or never. And Finn McLeod was definitely a *now* kind of guy.

* * *

A loud gasp from someone in the audience caused Allegra to pause as she finished her curtain call. The stage lights were so bright she couldn't see much past the edge of the stage, but Stephen was looking off to the left now, and some of the other dancers were pointing in that direction. She squinted and tried to adjust her eyes to the gloom beyond the footlights.

A murmur now, rumbling across the stalls, and then another louder collective intake of breath. Any residual applause died away. What on earth was happening out there?

Suddenly there was movement at the back of the auditorium—a couple of the security guards—and then the house lights came up. What was it? A fire? Then why hadn't the safety curtain come down? Why wasn't the alarm sounding? Allegra took a step and leaned forwards, trying to see what all the fuss was about.

That was when she saw the idiot dangling from the *outside* of one of the second tier boxes, one arm gripping the railing, one foot straining for the railing of the box below.

Insane! The man was literally insane.

Something else, too. Something that made her heart contract with an unwanted association. He was also fearless.

A lump rose in her throat. Tonight of all nights, some nutter had to go all Tarzan and remind her of *him*.

It might have been entertaining for those watching if the man hadn't slipped just then, only narrowly saving himself by balancing one foot, then the other on the edge of the Grand Tier balcony and hanging grimly onto the curved brass stem of one of the shaded lights nestled in the plasterwork.

That was when Allegra dropped the large bouquet she'd been holding and pressed her hands to her mouth.

There was only one man daft enough on this planet to try something so stupid.

Finn McLeod.

She held her breath as he nodded his greeting to the

shocked occupants of the box he'd landed on and continued his descent past them to the stalls.

Allegra didn't know what to do, what to think. Yes, she'd seen the story in that morning's paper about Finn and Natalie's split, but while that was current gossip to the rest of the nation, to her and Finn it was old news. It didn't change anything. So why was he here?

The sudden realisation of what he must have been doing—who he must have been watching—directly before he'd started his unconventional journey to the stalls hit her.

He'd seen her dance?

Now her hands moved to cover her face completely. If throwing herself at him on the beach hadn't been bad enough, he'd just witnessed her pouring the contents of her pathetic little heart out. It really was too humiliating.

The sounds of a scuffle and muffled shouting made her peel her fingers from her face. The security guards were now attempting to haul Finn off to the back of the auditorium where they'd be able to wrestle him down the stairs and out of view of the rubber-necking audience.

But Finn broke away and started to run towards the stage. Not for long, however. There were two of them and only one of him, and they hadn't just climbed down the outside of two balconies, so it didn't take them too long to restrain him again.

'Allegra!' he yelled as the guards dragged him to the top of the aisle.

The outraged whispering that had been steadily increasing in volume since Finn had hit the floor suddenly ceased.

'Crazed fan,' someone muttered behind her.

Allegra tried to get her tongue to work, but it just didn't want to cooperate.

They were almost there now, at the top of the stairs, and Finn would disappear in a few seconds, probably to spend the night in a police cell.

She took one last step forward. Stephen grabbed her arm but she shook him off.

'Wait!' she shouted and more than two thousand faces, which had all been facing the back of the auditorium, now swivelled to look at her. She swallowed.

'I know him,' she said, and her voice sounded breathless and scratchy, as if she hadn't used it for some time. 'It's okay.'

The two guards looked at each other and, while they weren't one hundred per cent focused on him, Finn slipped from their grasp. He stood up, straightened his terminally wrinkled clothing, patted one of the guards on the shoulder in a matey gesture of thanks and then began walking down the aisle towards her.

A bony hand grabbed at his sleeve and Finn almost brushed it away, but then he turned and saw its owner—an elderly lady with her white hair pulled tight into a bun at the top of her head. She thrust a cellophane-wrapped rose at him.

'Here, young man, I have a feeling you might be needing this.'

Finn nodded his thanks and carried on his journey, even though he knew a whole forest of red roses might not be enough to repair the damage he'd caused.

Allegra was standing right at the front of the stage, her hands loose by her sides. As he approached, she moved to the right of the stage, her back straight, until she was directly opposite the end of the aisle. He encountered a problem in the shape of the orchestra pit, but decided the most direct path was probably the best, and hopped over the barrier, narrowly missing a couple of the string section, and continued his journey.

It was awfully quiet, reminding him of when the crew had that instinct for when he was about to do something really stupid or really spectacular, and neither he nor they knew which until he did whatever he was going to do. Couldn't someone cough or rustle a sweet wrapper?

She looked so different like this, even close up. Instead of the messy ponytail he'd got used to, her hair was glossy and flowing. Her sun-kissed face was blanched with make-up. There were large dark sweeps of eyeliner both above and below her eyes and her mouth was blood-red. She almost seemed like another creature.

It was all wrong, wasn't it? Him coming here, making a fool of himself? He should just turn around and leave.

But then he spotted the tiny raised bumps on her arms and shoulders, insect bites that not even the stage make-up had been able to hide, and he began to smile.

He took his last step so he was standing at the footlights staring up at her. Her hand flew to her ribcage and stayed there. Complete silence blanketed the auditorium. She looked at him, fear and joy warring for pride of place in those large blue eyes.

He took a deep breath and resisted the urge to stuff his fists in his pockets. 'This grand enough for you?'

Allegra blinked and her mouth worked. 'Maybe,' she said finally.

He shook his head, not knowing what to say, where to start, so he handed her the rose and she clutched it to her torso with both hands.

'More flowers would have been better,' she said.

Finn shrugged, a crazy lightness surging up inside him. 'You know me—not a big planner. Tend to work with the re-sources at hand.'

Was that a glimmer of amusement in her eyes? He hoped so. Just the possibility gave him the guts to carry on.

'I'm sorry,' he said. 'Fell off a cliff again. Made a *really* stupid choice.'

There. A spark of hope in those blue irises. It lit a fire inside him and he hitched his mouth into a half smile, told her all about it with his eyes, and saw her receive and understand.

But he knew that wasn't enough. Some things needed to be said out loud.

He glanced over his shoulder briefly. Just hadn't expected so many straining ears in attendance when he finally got up the courage to say it.

'I love you, too.'

Allegra's lip quivered, and Finn got a horribly unfamiliar stinging sensation at the backs of his eyeballs.

'And I'm sorry I ran away. It was a stupid thing to do.'

She began to smile, slow warmth spreading her lips into a delicious curve. 'I know all about that,' she said softly. 'But running away sometimes has unexpected bonuses.'

Was it still quiet in the auditorium? Because Finn couldn't tell. The pounding in his ears had drowned it all out.

Allegra's gaze sharpened and became more intense. 'Tell me to jump, Finn.'

'Jump?' he said, suddenly very confused.

Too late to work out what she'd meant; she'd done it. With a bend of the knees and a push of the feet, she'd left the stage and a flying ballerina was heading straight towards him.

This time, however, he caught her.

And then he lowered her to the floor, making sure he kept her tightly in his arms. To have and to hold. Suddenly, he realised what a wonderful concept that was, what an amazing adventure that would be, so he used his lips to do something far more productive than talk. He used them to taste. To share his vision for the future. To promise.

Noise erupted around them. Finn opened half an eye and closed it again. Seemed as if Allegra Martin had just got her second standing ovation of the evening. But this time he was sharing it with her and that was fine by him. The noise around them only reflected what he was doing on the inside.

She wound her arms around his neck and pulled him closer,

pulled him deeper. He didn't resist. This was how it should be from now on. They were in this together now. Whatever crests and troughs life threw at them. What a fool he'd been.

'Allegra?'

She prised her lips from his and half-opened one eye. 'Mmm-hmm?'

'You mustn't let me be so stupid ever again.'

And she didn't, of course.

* * * * *

Mills & Boon® Hardback
February 2012

ROMANCE

An Offer She Can't Refuse	Emma Darcy
An Indecent Proposition	Carol Marinelli
A Night of Living Dangerously	Jennie Lucas
A Devilishly Dark Deal	Maggie Cox
Marriage Behind the Façade	Lynn Raye Harris
Forbidden to His Touch	Natasha Tate
Back in the Lion's Den	Elizabeth Power
Running From the Storm	Lee Wilkinson
Innocent 'til Proven Otherwise	Amy Andrews
Dancing with Danger	Fiona Harper
The Cop, the Puppy and Me	Cara Colter
Back in the Soldier's Arms	Soraya Lane
Invitation to the Prince's Palace	Jennie Adams
Miss Prim and the Billionaire	Lucy Gordon
The Shameless Life of Ruiz Acosta	Susan Stephens
Who Wants To Marry a Millionaire?	Nicola Marsh
Sydney Harbour Hospital: Lily's Scandal	Marion Lennox
Sydney Harbour Hospital: Zoe's Baby	Alison Roberts

HISTORICAL

The Scandalous Lord Lanchester	Anne Herries
His Compromised Countess	Deborah Hale
Destitute On His Doorstep	Helen Dickson
The Dragon and the Pearl	Jeannie Lin

MEDICAL

Gina's Little Secret	Jennifer Taylor
Taming the Lone Doc's Heart	Lucy Clark
The Runaway Nurse	Dianne Drake
The Baby Who Saved Dr Cynical	Connie Cox

Mills & Boon® Large Print

February 2012

ROMANCE

HISTORICAL

MEDICAL

Mills & Boon® Hardback

March 2012

ROMANCE

Roccanti's Marriage Revenge	Lynne Graham
The Devil and Miss Jones	Kate Walker
Sheikh Without a Heart	Sandra Marton
Savas's Wildcat	Anne McAllister
The Argentinian's Solace	Susan Stephens
A Wicked Persuasion	Catherine George
Girl on a Diamond Pedestal	Maisey Yates
The Theotokis Inheritance	Susanne James
The Good, the Bad and the Wild	Heidi Rice
The Ex Who Hired Her	Kate Hardy
A Bride for the Island Prince	Rebecca Winters
Pregnant with the Prince's Child	Raye Morgan
The Nanny and the Boss's Twins	Barbara McMahon
Once a Cowboy...	Patricia Thayer
Mr Right at the Wrong Time	Nikki Logan
When Chocolate Is Not Enough...	Nina Harrington
Sydney Harbour Hospital: Luca's Bad Girl	Amy Andrews
Falling for the Sheikh She Shouldn't	Fiona McArthur

HISTORICAL

Untamed Rogue, Scandalous Mistress	Bronwyn Scott
Honourable Doctor, Improper Arrangement	Mary Nichols
The Earl Plays With Fire	Isabelle Goddard
His Border Bride	Blythe Gifford

MEDICAL

Dr Cinderella's Midnight Fling	Kate Hardy
Brought Together by Baby	Margaret McDonagh
The Firebrand Who Unlocked His Heart	Anne Fraser
One Month to Become a Mum	Louisa George

Mills & Boon® Large Print

March 2012

ROMANCE

The Power of Vasilii	Penny Jordan
The Real Rio D'Aquila	Sandra Marton
A Shameful Consequence	Carol Marinelli
A Dangerous Infatuation	Chantelle Shaw
How a Cowboy Stole Her Heart	Donna Alward
Tall, Dark, Texas Ranger	Patricia Thayer
The Boy is Back in Town	Nina Harrington
Just An Ordinary Girl?	Jackie Braun

HISTORICAL

The Lady Gambles	Carole Mortimer
Lady Rosabella's Ruse	Ann Lethbridge
The Viscount's Scandalous Return	Anne Ashley
The Viking's Touch	Joanna Fulford

MEDICAL

Cort Mason – Dr Delectable	Carol Marinelli
Survival Guide to Dating Your Boss	Fiona McArthur
Return of the Maverick	Sue MacKay
It Started with a Pregnancy	Scarlet Wilson
Italian Doctor, No Strings Attached	Kate Hardy
Miracle Times Two	Josie Metcalfe